"Jess? I am sorry."

"About what?"

"Your daughter. Your husband. Your colt. You've had a rough time of it, and—"

"Please don't." The wind swept hair in front of her eyes, and she impatiently pushed it away. "The girls and I got along fine before you got here, and we'll be fine long after you go."

"Did I say you wouldn't? All I said was—"

"I really should get back to the house. Thank you for checking in on Honey."

Gage nodded, but he could've saved himself the effort as she was already out the door.

What was it with her always running away? Why wouldn't she talk to him? Why was she shutting herself off from the very practical fact that if she was going to run any kind of successful ranch, there was no way in Sam Hill she could ever do it on her own?

Catching his reflection in the mirror, he scowled. "What're you doing, man?"

But unfortunately, the stranger looking back at him had no more clue why he cared about Jess Cummings or her girls or her ranch than he did.

Dear Reader,

Welcome to the sixth and last book of THE STATE OF PARENTHOOD miniseries, Harlequin American Romance's celebration of parenthood and place. In this, our 25th year of publishing great books, we're delighted to bring you these heartwarming stories that sing the praises of the home state of six different authors and share the many trials and delights of being a parent.

If there's one time of the year that makes us think of home and family, it's Christmas. In Laura Marie Altom's *A Daddy for Christmas*, we meet Gage Moore, a Texan bull rider looking for peace—and redemption. What he finds is miles of blue Oklahoma sky and Jess Cummings, a single mom looking for a temporary ranch hand. It may seem as if Jess is the one who needs help, but working on her ranch and connecting with her two girls brings the spirit of Christmas home for Gage. And that holiday magic might just help make them a family.

There are five other books in this series: *Texas Lullaby* by Tina Leonard (June 08), *Smoky Mountain Reunion* by Lynnette Kent (July 08), *Cowboy Dad* by Cathy McDavid (August 08), *A Dad for Her Twins* by Tanya Michaels (September 08) and *Holding the Baby* by Margot Early (October 08). We hope you enjoyed every one of these romantic stories, and that they inspired you to celebrate where you live—because any place you raise a child is home.

Merry Christmas from all of us at American Romance!

Kathleen Scheibling
Senior Editor
Harlequin American Romance

A Daddy for Christmas
LAURA MARIE ALTOM

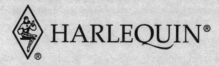

TORONTO • NEW YORK • LONDON
AMSTERDAM • PARIS • SYDNEY • HAMBURG
STOCKHOLM • ATHENS • TOKYO • MILAN • MADRID
PRAGUE • WARSAW • BUDAPEST • AUCKLAND

ISBN-13: 978-0-373-75237-9
ISBN-10:   0-373-75237-7

A DADDY FOR CHRISTMAS

ABOUT THE AUTHOR

After college (Go Hogs!), bestselling, award-winning author Laura Marie Altom did a brief stint as an interior designer before becoming a stay-at-home mom to boy/girl twins and a bonus son. Always an avid romance reader, when she found herself replotting the afternoon soaps, she knew it was time to try her hand at writing

When not immersed in her next story, Laura teaches reading enrichment at a local middle school. In her free time, she beats her kids at video games, tackles Mt. Laundry and of course, reads romance!

Laura loves hearing from readers at either P.O. Box 2074, Tulsa, OK 74101, or e-mail BaliPalm@aol.com.

Love winning fun stuff? Check out lauramariealtom.com!

Books by Laura Marie Altom

HARLEQUIN AMERICAN ROMANCE

*U.S. Marshals

For Mary Jane and Cathy Morgan.
Ladies, you are fun and talented and witty and
wonderful!! I love you!! Thanks for sharing
my ups, downs and everything in between!!

Chapter One

If Jess Cummings didn't act fast, the colt would have to be shot.

The heartrending sound of the young quarter horse's cries, the sight of blood staining his golden coat, made her eyes sting and throat ache. But she refused to give in to tears. For the colt's sake, for the girls' sake, but most of all, for Dwayne, to whom this land and its every creature had meant so much, Jess had to stay strong.

For what felt like an eternity, while the colt's momma neighed nervously behind the broken gate the colt had slipped through, Jess struggled to free the animal from his barbed-wire cage. Muscles straining, ignoring the brutal December wind's bite, she worked on, heedless of her own pain when the barbs pierced her gloves.

"You've got to calm down," she said, praying the colt her two girls had named Honey would somehow understand.

Not only didn't he still, but he also struggled all the harder. Kicking and snorting. Twisting the metal around his forelegs and rump and even his velvety nose that her daughters so loved to stroke.

The more the vast Oklahoma plain's wind howled, the more the colt fought, the more despair rose in Jess's throat. It was only two days before Christmas, and the holiday would be tough enough to get through. Why, *why,* was this happening now? How many times had she spoke up at grange meetings about the illegal dumping going on in the far southeast corner of her land? How many times had she begged the sheriff to look into the matter before one of her animals—or, God forbid, children—ended up hurt? For an inquisitive colt, the bushel of rotting apples and other trash lobbed along-side hundreds of feet of rusty barbed wire had made for an irresistible challenge.

"Shh..." she crooned, though the horse fought harder and harder until he eventually lost balance, falling onto his side. "Honey, you'll be all right. Every-thing's going to be all right."

Liar.

Cold sweat trickled down her back as she worked, and she promised herself that this time her words would ring true. That this crisis—unlike Dwayne's—could be resolved in a good way. A happy way. A way that didn't involve tears.

From behind her came a low rumbling, and the crunch of wheels on the lonely dirt road.

She glanced north to see a black pickup approach, kicking dust against an angry gunmetal sky. She knew every vehicle around these parts, and this one didn't belong. Someone's holiday company? Didn't matter why the traveler was there. All that truly mattered was flagging him or her down in time to help.

"I'll be right back," she said to Honey before charg-ing into the road's center, frantically waving her arms. "Help! Please, help!"

The pickup's male driver fishtailed to a stop on the weed-choked shoulder, instantly grasping the gravity of the situation. "Hand me those," the tall, lean cowboy-type said as he jumped out from behind the wheel, nodding to her wire cutters before tossing a weather-beaten Stetson into the truck's bed. "I'll cut while you try calming him down."

Working in tandem, the stranger snipped the wire, oblivious to the bloodied gouges on his fingers and palms, as Jess smoothed the colt's mane and ears, all the while crooning the kind of nonsensical comfort she would've to a fevered child.

In his weakened state, the colt had stopped struggling, yet his big brown eyes were still wild.

"Call your vet?" the stranger asked.

"I would've, but I don't have a cell."

"Here," he said, standing and passing off the wire cutters. "Use Doc Matthews?"

"Yes, but—" Before she could finish her question as to how he even knew the local horse and cattle expert, the stranger was halfway to his truck. Focusing on the task at hand, she figured on grilling the man about his identity later. After Honey was out of the proverbial woods.

"Doc's on his way," the man said a short while later, cell tucked in the chest pocket of his tan, denim work jacket. "And from the looks of this little fella, the sooner Doc gets here, the better."

Jess snipped the last of the wire from Honey's right foreleg, breathing easier now that the colt at least had a fighting chance. He'd lost a lot of blood, and the possibility of an infection would be a worry, but for the moment, all she could do was sit beside him, rubbing between his ears. "I can't thank you enough for stopping."

"It's what anyone would've done."

"Yes, well…" Words were hard to get past the burning knot in her throat. "Thanks."

The grim-faced stranger nodded, then went back to his truck bed for a saddle blanket he gently settled over the colt. "It's powerful cold out here. I'd like to go ahead and get him to your barn, but without the doc first checking the extent of his injuries—"

"I agree," she said. "It's probably best I wait here for him. But you go on to wherever you were headed. Your family's no doubt missing you."

His only answer was a grunt.

Turning the collar up on his jacket, eyeing her oversize coat, he asked, "Warm enough?"

"Fine," she lied, wondering if it was a bad sign that she could hardly feel her toes.

They sat in silence for a spell, icy wind pummeling their backs, Jess at the colt's head, the stranger at the animal's left flank.

"Name's Gage," he said after a while. "Gage Moore."

"J-Jess Cummings." Teeth chattering, she held out her gloved hand for him to shake, but quickly thought better. A nasty cut, rust-colored with dried blood, ran the length of his right forefinger. His left pinkie hadn't fared much better. Both palms were crisscrossed with smaller cuts, and a frighteningly large amount of blood. "You need a doctor yourself."

He shrugged. "I've suffered worse."

The shadows behind his eyes told her he wasn't just talking about his current physical pain.

"Still. If you'd like to follow me and Doc Matthews back to the house, I've got a first-aid kit. Least I can do is bandage you up."

He answered with another shrug.

"Some of those look pretty deep. You may need stitches."

"I'm good," he said, gazing at the colt.

Jess knew the man was far from *good,* but seeing as how the vet had pulled his truck and trailer alongside them, she let the matter slide.

"Little one," the kindly old vet said to Honey on his approach, raising bushy white eyebrows and shaking his head, "you've been nothing but trouble since the day you were born."

Black leather medical kit beside him, Doc Matthews knelt to perform a perfunctory examination. He wasn't kidding about Honey having been into his fair share of mischief. He'd given his momma, Buttercup, a rough breech labor, then had proceeded along his rowdy ways to gallop right into a hornet's nest, bite into an unopened feed bag and eat himself into quite a bellyache, and now, this.

"He going to be all right?" Jess was almost afraid to ask. "You know how attached the girls are. I don't know how I'd break it to them if—"

"Don't you worry," Doc said. "This guy's tougher than he looks. I'm going to give him something for pain, have Gage help settle him and his momma in my trailer and out of this chill. Then we'll get them back to the barn so I can stitch up the little guy and salve these wounds. After that, with antibiotics and rest, he should be right as rain."

Relieved tears stung her eyes, but still Jess wouldn't allow herself the luxury of breaking down.

"How'd you get all the way out here?" Doc asked her after he and Gage gingerly placed Honey and her still-agitated momma in the horse trailer attached to the vet's old Ford. He did a quick search for Jess's truck, or Smoky Joe—the paint she'd been riding since her sixteenth birthday.

In all the excitement, Jess realized she hadn't tethered Smoky, meaning by now, he was probably back at the barn. With a wry smile, she said, "Looks like I've been abandoned. You know Smoky, he's never been a big fan of cold or Honey's brand of adventure."

"Yup." Doc laughed. "Ask me, he's the smartest one in the bunch." Sighing, heading for his pickup with Matthews's Veterinary Services painted on the doors, he said, "Oh, well, hop in the cab with me, and we'll warm up while catching up."

"Shouldn't I ride in back with the patient?"

"Relax. After the shot I gave him, he'll be happy for a while, already dreaming of the next time he gives you and I a coronary."

"Should I, ah, head back to your place?" Gage asked.

"Nope," Doc said. "Martha wanted to keep you with us 'til after the holidays, but I figure now's as good a time as any for you and Jess to get better acquainted."

"Mind telling me what that's supposed to mean?" Jess asked once she and Doc were in his truck. She'd removed her gloves and fastened her seat belt, and now held cold-stiffened fingers in front of the blasting heat vents.

"What?"

"Don't act all innocent with me. You know exactly, *what*. Have you and my father been matchmaking again? If so, I—"

"Settle yourself right on down, little lady. Trust me, we learned our lesson after Pete Clayton told us you ran him off your place with a loaded shotgun."

"He tried kissing me."

"Can you blame him?" the older man said with a

chuckle. "If you weren't young enough to be my grand-daughter, you're pretty enough I might have a try at you myself."

Lips pursed, Jess shook her head. "Dwayne's only been gone—"

"Barely over a year. I know, Jess. We all know. But you're a bright and beautiful—and very much alive—young woman with two rowdy girls to raise. Dwayne wouldn't want you living like you do, with one foot practically in your own grave."

"As usual, you're being melodramatic. Me and the girls are happy as can be expected, thank you very much. I have no interest in dating—especially not another cowboy you and my daddy come up with."

"Understood," he said, turning into her gravel drive. "Which is why Gage's only in town to help you out around the ranch."

"What?" Popping off her seat belt, she angled on the seat to cast Doc her most fearsome glare.

"Simmer down. Everyone who loves you is worried. There's too much work here to handle on your own—especially with foaling season right around the corner. We've taken up a collection, and paid Gage his first few months' wages."

She opened her mouth to protest, but before getting a word in edgewise, Doc was holding out his hand to cut off her protestations.

"While you've been off checking fences this past week, your momma and my Martha have been fixing up the old bunkhouse. Gage is a good man. I've known his family since before he was born. More importantly, he's a damned hard worker, and will considerably lighten your load."

"But I couldn't possibly afford to—"

"Shh. Stop right there. Like I already said, whether you like it or not, the man's time has already been paid in full. Once spring rolls around and you're back on your feet after making a few sales, you'll have more than enough cash to support you and the girls and an invaluable hired hand."

The vet turned on the radio, tuning it to an upbeat country classic. From the looks of it, he and her father were taking another stab at matchmaking.

"What're you grinning about?" Jess asked, shooting him a sideways glare.

"Nothin' much," Doc said, keeping his eyes on the road. "Just looking forward to the holidays."

She snorted.

"What's the matter? Someone spit in your eggnog?"

"Let's just say that the sooner this holiday season is over, the better I'll feel."

GAGE SAT IN his truck's cab, wishing himself anywhere else on the planet. He'd known from the start this was a bad idea. He'd have been better off back at his cramped condo. At least there, he knew where he stood.

Though he couldn't hear words, Jess Cummings's animated body language spoke volumes. He wasn't wanted.

When his dad first broached the subject of helping a friend of a friend up in Mercy, Oklahoma, it'd seemed like a good idea. After all, what better way to help himself than by helping others? Now, however, he realized he should've asked a helluva lot more questions about the job.

"Well?" Doc asked outside Gage's window, causing him to jump. "You gonna sit there all day, or help me get our patient to the barn?"

"Mommy!"

Gage had just creaked open his truck door when two curly-haired, redheaded munchkins dashed from the covered porch of a weary, one-story farmhouse that was in as bad a need of paint as it was a new tin roof. They were followed by an older, gray-haired version of Jess.

"Hey, sweeties," said the woman he'd presumed was to be his new boss as she kneeled to catch both girls up in a hug.

The taller one asked, "Is Honey going to be okay?"

"He'll be fine," Jess said.

"Hi." The older woman smiled warmly, extending her hand. "I'm Georgia, Jess's mom. You must be Walter's boy, Gage."

"Yes, ma'am," he said, removing the hat he'd slapped back on. It'd been a while since Gage had lived in a small town, so he'd forgotten how fast news traveled. "Nice to meet you. Mom and Dad speak highly of your whole family."

"They were always favorites around here. It nearly broke my heart when your momma told me you were moving away. Of course, seeing how you were only two at the time, I'm not figuring the move gave you much cause for trouble."

"No, ma'am."

"Can you give me a hand?" Doc asked from the back of his trailer.

"Sure," Gage said, secretly relieved for having been rescued from small talk. He used to love to meet new folks—or, as was apparently the case with Georgia, get reacquainted with old friends—but lately, he just didn't have the heart.

"He's bleeding!" the taller of the two girls cried at her first sight of the colt. "Mommy! Do something!"

Tears streamed down the girl's cheeks while the younger girl, wide-eyed, with her thumb stuck in her mouth, clung to her mother's thigh.

"Hush now," Doc said. "Honey's a tough cookie. He looks bad, but trust me, Lexie, after Gage and I get him patched up, he'll be good as new."

"Promise?"

"Yup. Now how 'bout you and Ashley get some coats on, then meet me in the barn. I could use the extra hands."

"Is it okay, Mommy?"

"Of course," Jess said. "Honey will probably be glad you two are there."

While the girls scampered inside, Georgia asked her daughter, "Now that they're busy, tell me true. Is Honey really going to be all right?"

"Doc thinks so." Even from a good twenty feet away, the exhaustion ringing from Jess's sigh struck a chord in Gage. All his father and Doc had told him was that Jess was a widow very much in need of a helping hand. No one had said anything about there being kids in the picture. Then, as if there weren't already enough needy creatures on the ranch, an old hound dog wandered up, sending a mixed message with a low growl, but with his tail wagging.

"Don't mind him," Jess said, jogging over. "Taffy likes letting everyone know up front who's boss. Slip him a few table scraps every now and then, and you two will be fast friends."

Georgia had headed back in the house.

Gage, Doc and Jess entered the barn. While wind rattled time-worn timbers, the temperature was at least bearable compared to outside, and the air smelled good, and familiar of hay and oats and leather.

The three of them managed to set the colt on a fresh

straw bed in one of the stalls, then led his momma in beside him. Doc gave the colt a pat and said, "You know how Martha likes The Weather Channel. She says we're in for one heckuva storm."

"Ice or snow?" Jess asked.

"Starting off ice, switching to snow."

"Sounds fun," Jess said with a sarcastic laugh.

"Got plenty of firewood?" Doc asked.

Though she nodded, she didn't meet his gaze.

"See why I called you?" Doc asked Gage. "The girl lies through her teeth. Watch, what she calls *plenty* of wood will be a quarter rick too wet to give good heat."

"First off," Jess said, tugging the saddled horse Gage presumed was Smoky Joe in from the paddock and into a stall, "I'm not a girl, but a woman. And second, I do have enough sense to have covered the woodpile during the last rain. Third, Gage, I know you mean well, but maybe you coming here wasn't such a good idea."

"Gage," Doc said, "whatever she blows on about, don't listen. Now, would you mind running out to my truck and getting my bag?"

"Sure," Gage said, thrilled for yet another escape.

"And after that, please check the woodpile on the south side of the house. If it's not in healthy shape, Martha will have my hide."

HANDS ON HER HIPS, after Gage was out of earshot, Jess said to Doc, "I understand you and my parents and Lord knows who else you've got in on this plan to *save me* mean well, but seriously, Doc, I've been taking care of me and my girls just fine for a while now, and I resent like hell you and my father hiring some stranger to ride in here like a knight in shining armor."

"It's not like that," Doc said, "and kindly soften your voice. Your screech-owl-shrill tone is spooking Honey."

"Sorry," she said, "it's just that—"

"We're here," Lexie said with Ashley in tow. "What can we do?"

"Lots." Doc gave them a list of busywork that would serve the dual purpose of not only keeping them out of trouble, but also making them feel special.

"Here's your bag," Gage said, planting it at the vet's feet. "You need anything, I'll be around the side of the house, looking after the wood."

Nibbling her lower lip, Jess gave the man a five-minute lead, then waited 'til Doc seemed plenty distracted with Honey's stitches before heading outside herself.

It was only two in the afternoon, but it might as well have been seven at night. The sky glowered gray.

What Jess would like to do was join her mother in the kitchen, where she was no doubt nursing a pot of tea while gossiping on the phone with one of her many church friends. What Jess did instead was march around the side of the house toward her obviously lacking woodpile.

The smack-thunk of an ax splitting a log, and the halves hitting frozen ground, alerted her to the fact that her new *employee* was already hard at work. Her first sight of him left her mouth dry. In a word—*wow*. Even on a day like this, chopping wood got a person's heat up, and Gage had removed his coat, slinging it over a split-rail fence. The white T-shirt he wore hugged his powerful chest.

Fighting an instant flash of guilt for even thinking such a thing, she averted her gaze before saying, "Put your coat back on before you catch your death of cold."

He glanced up, his breath a fine, white cloud. "I'm plenty warm. How's Honey?"

"Better. Doc's working on his stitches. Looks like he'll be here a while, but for sure, the worst has passed."

"Honey's a lucky fella," Gage said, midsmack into another log, "that you came along when you did. How'd you even know to look for him all the way out there?"

"He's always been fascinated by that old trash pile. When he and his mom went missing, that's the first place I thought to look."

"Some of that trash didn't look so old." He reached for another log, causing his biceps to harden. Again, Jess found herself struggling to look away.

"No. That valley's always been a favorite dump site. Not sure why—or how—I'll ever stop folks from using it."

He grunted.

It'd been so long since she'd been around a man not old enough to be her father or grandfather, she wasn't sure what the cryptic, wholly masculine reply meant. Maybe nothing. A catchall for the more wordy, feminine version of *It's amazing how downright rude some people can be by littering on a neighbor's land.*

"You, um, really should put your coat back on," she said, telling herself her advice had nothing to do with the fact the mere sight of that T-shirt clinging to his muscular chest was making her pulse race. "Looks like freezing rain could start any minute."

Again, she got the grunt.

"Freezing rain's nothing to mess around with," she prattled on. "Once it starts, you'd better be sure you're where you want to be, because odds are, you just may be there a while."

"Ma'am," he said, gathering a good eight to ten quartered logs in his strapping arms and adding them to the already healthier pile, "no offense, but I grew up in north Texas. I know all about freezing rain."

Of course, you do. But do you have any idea how well those Wranglers hug your—

"Mommy!" Ashley cried, skidding to a breathless stop alongside her. "Gramma said if you don't get in the house, you'll catch a death."

Gage chuckled.

The fact that he apparently found not only her, but also her entire family amusing, reminded Jess why she'd even tracked him down. To ask him to leave.

"Please tell Grandma I'll be right in," she said to her daughter, giving the pom-pom of her green crocheted hat an affectionate tweak.

"'Kay." As fast as her daughter had appeared, she ran off.

"She's a cutie," Gage said.

"Thanks."

"Hope I'm not overstepping—" he reached for another log "—but Doc told me what happened to your husband. Must've been a comfort having your girls."

More than you'll ever know.

Something about the warmth in the stranger's tone wrapped the simple truth of his words around her heart. Throat swelling with the full impact of a loss that suddenly seemed fresher than it had in a long time, she lacked the strength to speak.

"Anyway," he continued, "just wanted to say sorry. You got a raw deal."

Lips pursed, she nodded.

"You should—" he nodded to the house "—go in."

Though she couldn't begin to understand why, the fact that he cared if she were cold irritated her to no end.

She'd come over to tell him thanks, but no thanks, she and her girls could handle working this ranch just fine on their own, and in a span of fifteen minutes he'd managed to chop more wood than she had in a month. Now, just as Dwayne used to, he was protecting her. Sheltering her from the worst an Oklahoma winter could dish out. Coming from her husband, her high-school sweetheart, the only man she'd ever loved, the notion had been endearing. Coming from this stranger, it was insulting.

The truth of the matter was that in a few months, once she could no longer afford to pay him, he'd be gone. Just like her husband. Then, there she'd be, once again struggling to make a go of this place on her own. But that was okay. Because, stubborn as she was, she'd do just that.

Oh, Jess knew the stranger meant well, but the bottom line was that she was done depending on anyone for survival. And make no mistake, out here, eking out a living from the land was a matter of day-to-day survival.

As a glowing bride, she'd still believed in happily ever afters. She now knew better. Loved ones could be snatched from you in a black second. Twisters could take your home. Learning life doesn't come with a guarantee had been one of Jess's most valuable lessons. It had taught her to appreciate every day spent with her daughters and parents and few friends. It had also taught her not to let anyone else in. Even if that someone was only an apparently well-meaning hired hand. For the inevitable loss of his much-needed help would hurt her already broken spirit far more than long days of working the ranch hurt her weary muscles.

"Look," she finally said, all the more upset by the fact that the freezing rain had started, tinkling against the tin roof and the rusted antique tiller Dwayne had placed at the corner of the yard for decoration. They'd had such plans for this old place. Dreamed of fixing it up, little by little, and restoring it to the kind of working outfit they'd both be proud of. "I'm not sure how to politely put this, so I'm just going to come right out and say it. You're, um, doing an amazing job with this wood, and there's no doubt I could always use an extra hand, but—"

"You don't want me here?"

"Well…" Jess didn't want to be rude to the man, but yeah, she didn't want him here.

"Tell you what," he said, not pausing in his work. "Doc and my dad are pretty proud of themselves for hooking us up, and—"

Her cheeks flamed. "They *what?*"

"I didn't mean it like *that,*" Gage said, casting her a slow and easy and entirely too handsome grin. "Just that I've needed a change of scenery and you've obviously needed a strong back. To a couple of coots like Doc and my old man, I suppose we must seem like a good pair."

"Oh. Sure." Now, Jess's cheeks turned fiery due to having taken Gage's innocent statement the wrong way.

"Back to what I was saying, how about I stay through the afternoon—just long enough to get you a nice stockpile of wood—then be on my way before the weather gets too bad? Doc won't even have to know I'm gone 'til I'm over the state line."

"You'd do that? Pretend to stay, for me?"

"Hell," he said with a chuckle, "if I'd stand out here all afternoon, chopping wood for you in the freezing cold, why wouldn't I do a little thing like leaving you on your own?"

His laughter was contagious, and for an instant,

Jess's load felt lightened. Only, curiously enough, her healthier woodpile had less to do with her improved mood than the warmth of Gage's smile.

Chapter Two

Only a few more hours, and Gage would be back on the road to Texas. He'd expected to feel good about the fact, but the lead in his gut felt more like guilt.

Jess needed him. He'd been raised never to turn his back on someone in need, and considering Jess's situation, Gage was pretty much honor-bound to do right by the down-on-her-luck widow and her brood. Hell, even the mangy old dog currently curled in front of the living room's crackling fire seemed to need him.

"Thanks," Gage said, accepting the third bowl of chili Jess's mom had shoved in front of him. The meal was delicious, but the straight-backed kitchen chair was about as comfortable as a cedar fence rail. Don't even get him started on the one rowdy munchkin jawing his ears off about Tyrannosaurus rex eggs, and the other not-so-rowdy—okay, downright hostile—munchkin shooting him laserlike death stares.

Georgia, on the other hand, made for pleasant enough company with her gentle chatter about the weather and her corn bread recipe and how her husband should be here just any minute to fetch her in his four-wheel drive. Gage missed his own mom. This Christmas would be tough on her—most especially without him there. But she had his father and many friends to help her through. He just couldn't bring himself to see her; she reminded him too much of Marnie.

Maybe he'd go home for her birthday in March.

Doc had long since finished up on Honey, calmed Buttercup and taken off to help his wife wrap gifts for their six grandkids. Gage would've been on his way, but seeing how Jess's mom was still hanging around, he was obliged to stay.

Georgia fixed herself a second bowl of chili, sprinkled it with Colby Jack, then dropped into a straight-backed chair alongside him. "Ray Hawkins worked miracles on that old bunkhouse stove. Gage, you should be snug as a bug out there all through this storm."

"Actually…"

"He's staying? Here? In the bunkhouse? That's where I play Barbies." Lexie shoved her chair back, and stomped from the room.

"Sorry," Jess said. "Ever since her dad…"

Gage knew well enough what she left unsaid. Ever since the girl's dad had died, she didn't cotton to any new men sniffing around her mom. Well, she'd be safe from him. He'd be leaving soon, and besides, with all he'd been through in the past few months, he certainly wasn't looking for a woman.

Granted, Jess was a fine-looking woman.

Tall, with a figure just right for holding. A long mess of fiery-red hair that suited what he'd imagined to be an equally hot temper. And then there were her eyes. Mostly gray with a tinge of blue. On a sunny day, would they match the sky?

Too bad he'd never know.

"Thank you, ma'am, for this meal," he said to Georgia.

"You're most welcome," she said, glowing from the

compliment. "From the looks of you, a winter's worth of home cooking will do you good."

"Yes, ma'am." He had lost weight, but hadn't realized it showed. Not that it mattered.

"Mister Gage," Ashley said, "did you know a T-rex could bite through somebody and kill them with just one chomp? He'd mash them, squirting out their blood all over the place—just like a Fruit Gusher."

"Ashley Grace Cummings," Georgia scolded. "Must you speak of such things at the dinner table?"

"It's true," the girl said, slathering enough butter atop a corn muffin that it looked more like a frosted cupcake. "I figured Mister Gage should know to be careful. Just in case he ever sees one."

"Thanks," he said with a nod. "You're right, you can never be too careful around those T-rex's. Especially where I'm from in Texas."

"Where's that?" Jess asked, pushing her chair back and standing. She hadn't even finished her first bowl of chili. Whereas he'd lost a few pounds, upon closer inspection, without her heavy coat, she looked scary thin.

"Dallas. T-rexes on every corner. Good thing Miss Ashley, here, told me to watch out, or I'd be someone's dinner."

"I hope a T-rex does get you." Peeking around the corner from the living room into the kitchen was Lexie, wearing a satisfied smile. "At least then, you wouldn't be here."

"Lexie!" Georgia and Jess apologized on the girl's behalf, but Gage shrugged off their concern. It was all right. He and Lexie had more in common than she could ever possibly know. As such, he'd cut the kid some slack. More than a few times lately, he'd caught himself just short of railing on some poor waitress who'd botched his order. Or his manager for booking too many public appearances when Gage had specifically asked for none.

Jess's ranch would have been a wonderful place to hide.

Spend downtime nursing emotional wounds with hard work and—

"Heavens," Georgia said, glancing toward the porch at the sound of an unholy crash. "What was that?"

The back door burst open.

A red-faced, burly man dressed in a flannel shirt and denim overalls looked right at Gage, introduced himself as Jess's father, Harold, and said, "It's a darned good thing you're sticking around for a while because, judging by the mess I just made of my truck, you're gonna want to stay put."

SURVEYING THE DAMAGE her father had done to her porch rail, Jess didn't even try suppressing a groan.

This was a bad joke, right?

Like her home wasn't already ramshackle enough.

"Sorry, doodlebug," her father said beneath the porch's tin roof, kissing her cheek. He practically had to shout to be heard above the clattering ice. "Just as soon as this weather clears, I'll be over to fix the damage. With Gage's help, shouldn't take much longer than an afternoon."

"Th-that's all right, Dad." Arms crossed, teeth chattering, Jess glanced Gage's way. He wasn't going to go back on his word, was he? And tell her dad he wouldn't be staying? "You couldn't have helped it." The driveway was completely ice-slicked and her dad had simply lost control.

"Are you hurt?" Georgia asked, worry creasing her brow.

"Whoa!" nine-year-old Lexie said, off the porch and sliding on the icy drive in her pink snow boots. "Grandpa, you did a movie stunt!"

"I love you," Ashley said, pouring on the sweetness by hugging her grandfather's legs. "I'm glad you didn't get hurt from your movie stunt."

"I'm fine," he said, kissing Georgia.

"Think we need to stay here tonight?" his wife asked.

"Probably," he said with a sigh, "but if we do, who's going to look after the dogs?"

"Yeah," Jess prodded, yet not without a pang of guilt. "You can't forget about the dogs." *Just like I can't forget that if only you two would leave, so would Gage.* What kind of daughter was she? Wishing her parents out into this storm?

"We'll be fine," Jess's dad reassured. "In case we can't make it over, I brought the girls' presents. But we're going to have to hustle to unload, then get back on the road."

"Okay," Georgia said, already heading inside. "Let me get my coat, and I'll be right out to help."

"Wanna bet it takes her a good ten minutes to get back out here?" Jess's dad asked Gage with a good-natured grin.

"Wouldn't surprise me," Gage replied.

Georgia was back outside in five minutes. After a flurry of rushing back and forth with packages—little Ashley excited about each one, Lexie more reserved, almost as if she were trying to hide her excitement—Jess waved her parents on their way, saying a quick prayer for their safety.

The second her father's truck's brake lights cleared the drive, Ashley suggested, "Let's open all of Gramma and Grandpa's presents!"

"N-nope," Jess said, teeth chattering while she ushered the girls inside. "N-not until Christmas morning. But thanks for the idea. I think since I'm a grown-up, I'll go ahead and open mine now."

"That's not fair!" Ashley bellowed.

Laughing, Jess ruffled her youngest daughter's hair.

"Mom," Lexie asked, "can we watch a movie?"

"D-do the dishes first," Jess said.

"But—"

"Lexie..." Jess warned.

"She's a handful," Gage said after the girls had traipsed inside.

"T-tell me about it."

He chuckled, then stuck his hand out from under the porch's shelter, letting ice coat his palm. "This is bad. Probably the worst I've seen. Got any tire chains?"

"I d-don't th-think so," she said through teeth chattering so bad it was hard to speak. "I-if w-we do, they're in th-the b-barn."

"I'll look, you get back in the house."

"B-but..."

"Go," he said, pointing to the front door. "The longer you stand out here arguing, the longer it's going to take me to get on the road."

Famous last words.

Fifteen minutes later, through the living room curtains, Jess watched Gage slide rusty steel chains around his tires. But about five seconds after having put his truck in gear and backing up to test the traction, even through the window, she heard a metallic snap.

After turning off his truck, Gage hopped out to inspect, only to promptly fall on his behind.

Jess snatched a quilt from the back of a rocker, wrapped it around her shoulders, then dashed outside. Into driving wind and ice, she shouted, "You okay?"

"Fine. Unless you count wounded pride." Scrambling to his feet and gingerly rising to his full height, he brushed ice from the backside of his jeans. "Got any welding gear? It won't be pretty, but I'm good enough to jury-rig these to hold 'til the state line."

Freezing rain still fell, tinkling, tinkling, coating the world in sparkling wonder. The scene was beautiful, yet the lead in her stomach filled her with dread. Both tire chains had snapped. Gage could hardly stand. It would be downright suicidal expecting him to go anywhere until the storm cleared. "Stay."

"Excuse me?" Using his boots as skates, he slid onto the porch. "A few hours ago, you wanted nothing more than for me to go."

"I-I do. But not now. Stay—at least until the roads clear. Dad called to tell me they made it home okay, but it was rough going. If something happened to you…" Her throat tightened. "Gage, you strike me as a smart guy. You know driving in this would be foolhardy."

Shivering, blowing on cupped hands, he nodded. "But so is sticking around where I'm not wanted." A faint grin told her he was trying to lighten the moment. His hooded eyes told her he was still willing to go— no matter the weather.

"I'm sorry, all right? Earlier, I wasn't thinking clearly, but n-now…" The cold was again becoming unbearable. "P-please, as a f-favor… Stay."

He reached out to her, almost as if on the verge of setting his broad hands to her trembling shoulders. But then, having apparently thought better, he shoved them into his pockets. "This mess won't last forever. Christmas will come and go. I'll hole up in the bunkhouse for a few days, then be on my way."

"Thanks," she said with a nod. "That sounds good."

"I do have one question for you," he called over his

shoulder while carefully stepping to his truck, using the bed's rails for support while grabbing an ice-coated black duffel.

"Sh-shoot."

After walking back on the porch, he asked, "Why, when from all I've seen, you could clearly use a helping hand, are you so hell-bent on running this place on your own?"

"It's p-personal," she answered, bristling, and turned toward the house's softly glowing lights.

"It's personal to me that there's no way you can adequately handle this operation yourself. I hate seeing horses suffer, and with foaling season right around the corner, you—"

"M-my horses *aren't* suffering." Damn her chattering teeth. She hated having weaknesses, let alone showing them. Squaring her shoulders, despite driving freezing rain sounding as if it might bore holes through the tin roof, she added, "M-my animals are f-family. I would n-never—"

"Do you realize that if you weren't so strapped for time, Honey wouldn't have had the opportunity to escape?"

"You're blaming what happened to Honey on me?" Anger burned through her, providing momentary relief from the cold.

"Not at all, I'm just—"

She didn't hear the rest of what he'd said because as swiftly as she could manage with the long quilt flapping around her legs, she'd escaped his accusatory stare for her home's welcoming warmth.

GAGE SHOVED OPEN the bunkhouse door only to be hit by a wall of heat. Bless Doc. Before leaving, he must've made a fire in the cast-iron stove.

Removing his hat, Gage hooked it over the footboard of a white, wrought-iron bed. He pressed down on the quilt-covered mattress, testing the give. Not too hard or soft. Good. He could use a decent night's rest.

Setting his bag on the worn wood floor, wincing at the handle's bite on his roughed-up hands, he shrugged off his jacket, hung it on a row of brass hooks on the wall. He'd seen a lot of bunkhouses in his day, but this one beat all. Frilly, flowery curtains hung over three wide-paned windows that gazed out on a rolling pasture—currently a grayish-white instead of the customary green. Paintings dotted the walls with color. Mountains, flowers and horses were the predominant themes.

An older-model TV sat on a dresser, wearing a rabbit-ear antennae that looked like a hat. A bookshelf nestled alongside the dresser held a range of worn paperbacks and a few stacks of assorted magazines.

A narrow door to the left of the bed led to a small bathroom complete with thick, white towels and a claw-foot tub.

Gage looked around and groaned, running his hands through his hair.

Well… Here he was. Home sweet home—at least until the roads cleared.

He sat down in an oak rocker in front of the stove.

You're blaming what happened to Honey on me?

Elbows on his knees, resting his chin on cold, fisted hands, Gage willed Jess's question from his weary brain.

Honestly? Yeah, maybe a small part of him did blame her. Why was she—like his sister—so damned stubborn to ask for help? How many times could Marnie have turned to him? Leaned on him for support? Instead, she'd insisted on handling the mess *he'd* put her in all by herself.

Impossible. That's what women were.

He'd headed up here with the express intention of making sense of his life, and here he was, more confused than ever.

Leaning forward, he grabbed the poker from a stand of fireplace tools. His fingers were so numb, the flame's heat stung. He jabbed at the crackling pile of logs and glowing coals. Just his luck that he'd apparently jumped from one emotion-packed fire into another.

A knock sounded at the door.

"Come in," he called out, voice wary.

The older of Jess's girls stumbled in with the cold.

"Your mom know where you are?" he asked.

"She's taking a nap."

"So that'd be *no?*"

"*No*, what?" she asked, standing there, dripping water all over the floor.

Frowning, Gage turned his attention from her back to the fire. "What brings you all the way out here?"

"This is *my* house," she said, wagging a pink, briefcase-size box that had *Barbie* emblazoned across the front. "Me and my dolls live here—*not* you."

A glance over his shoulder showed a determined set to her jaw and eyes so squinty it was a wonder the kid's freckles weren't glowing. "Trust me, Tater Tot, I'll be gone before you know it."

"Good." After tossing her dripping pink case onto his bed, she crossed her arms.

"Well? Is there something else I can help you with?"

"You're in my way."

"Of what?"

"That's where I set up my ranch." She pointed to the fieldstone stove surround. "My dolls camp by the fire."

"Don't you think it's a little hot right now?"

Lips pursed, she rolled her eyes.

Flipping open the latch on her box, out came piles of doll clothes and hats and tiny shoes that'd be hell on his back if she inadvertently left one behind. "My dolls are Sooners. We learned in school that's what the prairie people were who got their land first before the land rush started."

"Wasn't that cheating?" Gage couldn't resist asking.

His question earned him a scowl. "If you'd've come here, even when the land rush officially started, they probably wouldn't have let you stay."

"Fair enough," he said over his shoulder. "Seeing how I'm a Texan, I wouldn't have wanted any smelly old Oklahoma land."

"Hey," she said, bristling, "our state's not smelly."

"Duh. I was making a joke. You're a kid. I thought you knew how to laugh?"

"I do. But only with people I like."

"Oh." Well, she put him in his place. What would it take to get a brokenhearted tadpole like this girl to laugh again?

"It's a good thing my dolls are prairie people, 'cause they don't have a house or furniture."

"Don't you at least have a covered wagon for them to stay in when it rains?"

"Nah. But that'd be really cool."

The bunkhouse door opened, ushering in a powerful cold wind and one more munchkin. "There you are," the girl said to her sister. Gage knew their names, but had forgotten which one was which.

"Who's Ashley and who's Lexie?"

"I'm Lexie and I'm oldest," said the tall one with hornet-mean eyes.

"I'm Ashley and I'm smarter," said Shorty. The kid

helped herself—sneakers and dinosaur-themed rain-coat dripping—to bouncing on his bed. "Did you know the biggest dinosaur egg ever found was as big as a football?"

"You're *sooooooo* dumb," Lexie said.

"You're dumb," said Dino Girl.

"You're dumber."

"You're dumbest!"

"You're dumb to infinity!" Chin high, Lexie wore a victor's snide smile. "I win."

Gage stood. "I don't mean to get in the way of this deep conversation, but would y'all mind taking this somewhere else? I could really use a nap, and, Ashley, you're dripping all over my bed."

"Thought you were leaving?" Lexie asked, her fury back on him. "I want to play with my dolls."

Sighing, Gage squeezed his eyes closed for just a sec, praying that when he opened them, the munchkins would be gone.

No such luck.

"Look, kiddos," he said, "I just think that—"

The bunkhouse door burst open.

This time, along with plenty of ice and cold wind, Jess stepped into his suddenly overcrowded space. The wind caught the door, slamming it behind her. Leaving an even bigger puddle than either of her girls, she settled gloved hands on her hips before scolding, "Just what in the world are you two doing?"

"I wanna play with my dolls," Lexie whined, "but *he's* in my way." Three guesses as to who the kid pointed to, and the first two didn't count.

"I wanted someone to play with," Ashley said to her mom, "and you were sleeping, and Lexie's too mean."

"Am not!"

While Lexie stuck out her tongue at her sister, Gage fought the urge to cover his ears with his hands. How in the hell had his life come to this? Stuck out in the middle of nowhere with three bellyaching females and a sky that refused to quit *falling*.

"Both of you scoot your fannies back to the house." In a stern, momlike pose, Jess waved a hand in the general direction of their home's front porch.

"But I wanna stay and play dolls," Lexie argued. "And *he's* in my way."

"Lex…" Jess warned, her tone no-nonsense.

Proving she *was* the smart one, Ashley scooted off the bed and hit the ground running.

Lexie aimed for the door, as well, but not without first shooting him a classic little-kid dirty look after scooping up her doll stuff and shoving it in the box.

"Lex," Jess said, hands back on her hips, "apologize to our guest."

"No." The girl raised her chin.

Mmmph. Talk about sass… It took everything Gage had in him not to march the kid into the bathroom and wash her mouth out with soap.

"Lexie Margaret Cummings, get your rear to your room."

Thankfully, the girl did as she'd been told.

Once Gage and Jess were on their own with nothing between them but the storm's rooftop racket and the child's lingering chill, he cleared his throat. "That was, um…"

"Infuriating?" Sitting hard on the edge of his bed, tugging off a green crocheted cap that matched her younger daughter's, she sighed. "Ever since—well, since my… I mean, her father—"

"Jess…" Swallowing a knot that had formed right

about the time he'd seen the pain Lexie's defiant behavior had caused in her mother's eyes, Gage cleared
his throat. "It's all right. I'll be gone soon, so there's no
need to explain." *I've got enough of my own emotional
baggage. I don't need to be taking on anyone else's.*
"What happens between you and your girls... It's...
Well, it's really none of my business."

"I know," she said, staring into the fire merrily crackling behind the woodstove's open doors, no doubt completely unaware of how beautiful she was. Vulnerable.
Fragile. In another time, the Texas gentleman in him
would have felt obligated to somehow help. Now? He
had nothing left to give. She sighed. "I wouldn't have
even said anything, but you seem to be her latest target."

Shifting his weight from one leg to the other, he
raised an eyebrow. "Target?"

"She's bitter about what happened. To her dad, I
mean. Any man close to his age who steps foot on the
property, she seems to systematically drive away."

"Which is another reason you don't need help with
the ranch?"

He took her silence as an affirmation.

"You should take a firm hand with her. Show her
who's boss."

She snorted. "Easier said than done. It's not that
simple."

"I can imagine." He was having a tough enough time
dealing with Marnie's death, and all he had to tackle
was his own guilt-laced grief. He couldn't fathom
having to get a couple of kids through that particular
brand of pain, as well.

But then Ashley and Lexie hadn't played a pivotal
role in their father's passing, as he had with his sister's.
Sure, he'd been told by everyone he knew that what

happened hadn't been his fault, but inside—where it counted—he knew better.

Her stare still fixed on the fire, Jess said, "My parents…and Doc—they're right. I do need help. I am stubborn. Lexie is a mess…." As her words trailed off, the freezing rain pounded all the harder on the tin roof. "I'm sorry. I really should check on the girls—and Honey."

"I'll see after the colt."

"No, really, for all practical purposes, you're our guest. I can't further impose on you by—"

"I said I'll look after the colt."

For the briefest of moments, Jess's gaze met his. Gage sensed so much simmering just beneath her public facade. What would it take to expose all of her fears until bringing them to light burned them away? Not that he was the person to tackle the job. He wasn't in any shape to help her, and even if he were, she obviously didn't want his help.

"Thank you," she said, rising from his bed, slipping on her cap, tucking it low around her ears. How could a grown woman manage to look so adorable?

"No problem."

"What time do you eat breakfast?" she asked, having almost reached the door.

"Usually around seven, but—"

"I'll have something fixed for you by then." The vulnerability she'd earlier shown had been replaced by an impenetrable mask. The chilly set to her mouth made the night's brutal cold seem downright balmy.

"Don't go to any trouble."

"I'm not."

She'd opened the door on the howling wind and stepped outside when he called, "Jess?"

"Yes?" she asked, tone wary.

"I am sorry."

"About what?" Her cheeks and nose were already turning pink from the cold.

"Your daughter. Your husband. Your colt. You've had a rough time of it, and—"

"Mr. Moore, please don't." The wind swept hair in front of her eyes, and she impatiently pushed it away. "The girls and I got along fine before you got here, and we'll be fine long after you go."

"Did I say you wouldn't be fine? All I said was—"

"I'm sorry. I don't mean to be rude, but I really should get back to the house. Thank you for agreeing to check in on Honey."

He nodded, but he could've saved himself the effort as she was already out the door.

What was it with her always running away? Why wouldn't she talk to him? Why was she shutting herself off from the very practical fact that if she were going to run any kind of successful ranch, there was no way in Sam Hill she could ever do it on her own? And what was she planning on doing about her kid? Lexie. The girl was obviously in a bad way.

Catching his reflection in the dresser's mirror, he scowled. "What're you doing, man?"

Too bad for him, the stranger looking back at him had no more clue why he cared about Jess Cummings or her little girl or her ranch than he did.

Chapter Three

"Mommy? Is he dead?" Ashley poked her thumb in her mouth and grasped Jess's hand.

"No, hon, Mr. Moore's fine. Just sleeping." Six in the morning on Christmas Eve, freezing rain clattering like a million dimes on the barn's tin roof, Gage Moore was sound asleep in Honey and Buttercup's stall, using a hay bale for a pillow and a saddle blanket for warmth. The air in the barn was more bearable than outside, but still cold enough to see your breath. It took a good man to sleep in conditions like this just to look after a horse—it was something her husband would have done.

"Thought he was leaving?" Lexie asked, arms crossed, shooting their guest her customary glare. Jess's stomach tightened. What was she going to do about the girl? She used to be all smiles and full of life. Now, she was sullen and argumentative and wielded her pout like a weapon.

"Sweetheart, he is leaving, but the roads are a mess, so he can't exactly get to Texas. Not only that, but it's almost Christmas. Don't you think the charitable thing to do would be to at least be polite? After all, he did come here to help us."

"We don't need help."

The girl's demeanor softened when she knelt to stroke Honey's muzzle.

Buttercup neighed.

"Hey, girl," Jess crooned, keeping her voice low so as not to wake Gage. "Your baby's looking much better."

"Mommy?" Ashley asked.

"Yes, hon?"

"What's chair-it-abble mean?"

Jess patted the mare's rust-colored rump. "When someone does something nice for someone not because they have to, but because they want to."

"Oh." The little girl took off her coat, lightly settling it over Gage.

Whereas moments earlier, Jess's stomach had been knotted with worry for her eldest daughter, her heart lightened at her youngest girl's good deed. Though her green coat barely covered the large man's shoulder, the generosity of the child's good intentions filled the whole barn.

"You're lame," Lexie said, standing and heading for the door. "Because of him, our Christmas is ruined."

Jess sighed.

Why was it that just when she thought everything might be all right, something—or, in this case, *somebody*—brought her hopes crashing down?

"We should just cancel Christmas."

"Lexie, stop. Just stop, or Santa's bringing you nothing but a bag of switches."

"Good. Because I don't even believe in Santa."

"He's real!" Ashley shouted.

"Shut up!" Lexie shouted back.

Gage shifted and groaned. "What's going on?"

"Lexie Margaret Cummings," Jess said, hands on her

hips, "that's enough out of you. Apologize to your sister, then march straight to your room."

The girl's apology consisted of sticking out her tongue before taking off for the barn's door.

"Lexie!" Jess shouted. "Lexie! Get back here this instant, before—"

"Let her go," Gage said, stepping up behind her.

Ashley had her thumb back in her mouth as she quietly watched her sister go. "Mommy?"

"Yes, sweetie?"

"How come Lexie hates me?"

Jess pulled her youngest into a hug. "She doesn't hate you, pumpkin. I think she hates—" Chest aching from bearing the weight of both of her girls' emotional pain, Jess couldn't go on. Not here, with Gage looking on. What her daughter hated, but was too emotionally immature to vocalize, was most likely every man on the planet for living when her daddy had died. How did Jess make Lexie see it was all right for her to go on with her life? To be happy again and run and skip and play jump rope? But then how did she teach her daughter all of that when Jess didn't begin to know herself?

Behind her, Gage cleared his throat. "Honey made it just fine through the night. He's a scrapper, Jess.... Just like your little girl."

With everything in her, Jess wanted to fight him, this virtual stranger. After all, what did he know about her daughter or anything else? But he had spent the night in the frigid barn, sleeping alongside the dearest of colts. That kindness deserved something, even if all she had in her was to bite her tongue.

She swallowed hard. "Thank you."

"It's the truth. Lexie's just going through a phase that—"

"I meant, thank you for staying with Honey. Lexie's my problem. I appreciate your advice, but—"

"Mind my own business?" His mouth's grim set told her that once again, where he was concerned, she'd gone too far. She didn't mean to be short with him, but couldn't seem to help herself.

"I'm sorry," she said to Gage, squeezing Ashley's hand. The girl was staring up at her, big brown eyes taking everything in. "Hungry?"

"Starved," he answered. "It's been a while since Georgia's chili."

Jess summoned a cautious smile, then said, "I'm not half as good a cook as my mother, but if you're feeling brave, I'd be happy to whip up something simple like pancakes and bacon."

"MMM…" GAGE SAID with a groan, pushing back his plate. "Your mom lied," he said to Ashley. "She's a good cook."

Cheeks puffed with an oversized bite of pancakes, the girl nodded.

He hadn't had much of an appetite lately, but something about Jess's welcoming country kitchen made him want to eat, and it felt good having his belly full.

The blue linoleum floor was peeling in the corners, and the whitewashed cabinets might be in as desperate need of paint as the home's exterior, but the yellow flowered curtains covering fogged-over paned windows were ruffled and feminine and pretty, and the abundance of thriving houseplants told him that despite the home's shabby appearance, it was indeed a home. Gut feel told him Jess was an expert at transforming life's lemons into sweet lemonade. If only he'd learned the same.

Jess had taken Lexie a plate to her room, leaving him on his own alongside Ashley at the round oak kitchen table.

"Guess what?" she asked, half a canned peach in her chubby fingers. The syrup dripped down her wrist.

"You might want to—" He gestured for her to use her napkin.

Instead, she licked the dripping mess.

Gage winced.

"What's wrong?" the girl asked. "I haven't even told you what I was gonna tell you yet. And it wasn't awful."

"Oh," he said, striking a solemn pose. "Sorry. Please, carry on with what you were about to say before I so rudely interrupted."

Her grin warmed him more effectively than Jess's fragrant coffee.

"Okay," Ashley said, "did you know a *brakeeo-sore-us* is as long as two school buses and tall as four buildings?"

"I did not know that. Thank you."

"You're welcome. Here—" She plopped a second peach half on his plate. "I'm full, so you can have this."

"Um, thanks." Though the fruit swam in a sea of buttery syrup, and Gage had never been big on mixing his foods, seeing how Ashley stared at him expectantly, he went ahead and forced a bite. "Mmm… Thanks."

"You're welcome." She pushed back her chair and leaped to her feet. "See ya."

"Where are you going?"

"I've got to work on my pictures for Santa. Daddy always said if you left cookies and some pretty drawings for Mrs. Claus's 'frigerator, he'd leave more toys."

"Your dad sounded very smart."

"He was. I loved him lots." She pushed her chair in and took her plate to the sink. "Bye."

Just as Ashley went out, Jess headed back in. "I hope she didn't yak your ears off."

Chuckling, he checked if his ears were still attached. "All good."

She laughed, a really heartfelt laugh that made him feel funny inside. Not *ha-ha* funny, but strange as it sounded even to him, proud to have made her smile. "Is she off to work on her pictures for Mrs. Claus?"

"Yes, ma'am." He rose, grabbing his plate and the butter dish before heading for the sink. "Cute custom."

"I love that she still believes."

"Yeah. It is nice." Gage used to believe in magic. Then he'd urged Marnie into taking up with Deke, and nothing had ever been the same.

"You don't have to do that," she said, stopping him halfway to the sink and reaching for his dish.

"I know I don't *have* to," he pointed out, "but the rule in my house is that whoever cooks doesn't have to clean."

"I think I like your house," she said, backing away. "By all means…go for it. The scrub pad and soap are under the sink."

"Not that I'm complaining," he added while Jess refilled her coffee mug, "but what's gotten into you to actually accept help?"

She grimaced. "Have I sounded that bad?"

"Pretty much."

"Sorry." Jess sat at the table, munching a piece of bacon she'd snatched from a plate on the counter by the stove. "It's just with Lexie's mood swings and Ashley's penchant for mischief—not to mention Honey's—I've been snappier than usual."

"No biggie. Especially after what you've been through."

"Don't," she said quietly.

"What?"

"Make excuses." She sipped her coffee, taking her time finding just the right words. She was tired of coming across as bitchy when there was so much more behind her needing him to leave. There were Lexie's issues and her own need to make the ranch as perfect as she and Dwayne had always dreamed it would be. Moreover, deep inside, when she was alone in her bed in the cold still of night, only then did she acknowledge the terror she felt at the thought of depending on anyone ever again.

Hugging her fingers around her mug, she said haltingly, "I-I hate when everyone blames my every problem on my husband's death. Dwayne died last fall. I should be over it, you know? Not that I ever want to forget him, just that my never being able to fit enough work into any given day shouldn't have anything to do with his being gone."

"Sure," he said, rinsing and then drying the frying pan. "I get it. But—and please, don't take this the wrong way—you're a damned fool if you think you can handle an operation this size on your own." He reached for a plate to scrub. "Truth is, you could really use a few more men…or women. I don't get why you feel this compulsion to run this place all by your lonesome."

How many times had her parents and Doc said the same thing? How many times had Jess tried telling them she didn't know. Only she did. And telling anyone would make him or her believe her certifiable.

"You're right," she confessed. "I do need help, and plenty of it. But so far, the ranch hasn't profited like I'd hoped. Once we're out of the red, I'll hire lots of hands. But now… It just isn't feasible."

ISN'T FEASIBLE?

A couple hours later, scooting across the ice rink that had become her yard with socks over her sneakers to help with traction, Jess wished she had an extra leg with which to kick herself. How dumb had that sounded? Especially in light of the fact that Gage's services were already paid for.

With both girls and the dog sharing a rare moment of unity over cookies and milk and a Disney movie, Jess was midway to the barn to check on Honey when she got a little too cocky with her speed and her feet went out from under her.

Her resulting yelp echoed across the frozen yard.

She tried scrambling back onto her feet, but only ended up sliding.

Lying back, she stared up at the gray sky. Swell. Just swell.

"Need a hand?" called an all-too-familiar masculine voice from the barn.

"I probably do," she conceded to Gage with a weary smile, "but I'm not all that sure you can make it out here."

"I s'pose I could throw you a rope." He was leaning against the doorjamb, a grin tugging at the corners of his lips.

"Don't do me any favors," she sassed, scrambling to her knees, surely resembling a drunken crab.

He snorted, making a valiant stab at reaching her. At least until he fell, too.

"Holy crap, that hurt," he complained, rubbing his backside.

"You okay?" She was back on her knees, crawling toward him.

"Yet again, I'm thinking everything but my pride will be fine." He tried getting to his feet, but this particular stretch of the drive was sloped and enough snow had fallen during the night to create a drift. More freezing rain had coated it, transforming an already bad situation into a disaster.

"Here, let me try getting to you." She made it, only to start sliding.

"Give me your hand."

Jess did, and he caught her just before she started sliding into the icy abyss—well, really more of a dip, but considering how cold the ice felt seeping through the seat of her jeans, she preferred not to be outside a second longer than necessary.

"Hang tight and I'll pull you up." Gage tugged her arm, pulling her along the ice, and for a split second it hurt, but then she was laughing and he was laughing and she was resting against him, clinging to his jacket, relishing his warmth…his strength.

"Th-thanks," she said, teeth chattering.

"Come on, let's get you inside." He hammered his boot heels into the ice, then pushed up with his powerful legs. His arms cinched her to him, and while she should've been put off by his proximity, what she really felt was safe. Protected. And for the fleeting moments it took to reach higher, flatter ground, she rejoiced in the emotions. But then Gage released her and struggled to his feet. Ever the gentleman, he offered her his gloved hands and for the briefest of seconds, she accepted them, telling herself it wasn't a tingle of awareness flooding her with heat, but the barn's warmer air.

"That was, um, good thinking," she said, once again

stable on her feet now that they were on the barn's dirt floor. "Thanks again."

"No problem."

As Gage headed for Honey's stall, Jess watched him. The breadth of his shoulders under his coat. The smattering of ice and snow clinging to his hair. He smelled fresh and clean, like the straw he'd spent the night on. But there'd also been a trace of the bacon they'd had for breakfast. The syrup. The coffee. The smells of normalcy—it seemed a lifetime since she'd last experienced them.

Frustration balled in her stomach, building into a wall of panic she wasn't sure how to break down. Gage Moore had to go. Now. This second. Only it was Christmas Eve, and judging by the clatter on the tin roof, additional freezing rain had arrived instead of Santa and his reindeer.

"You're a sweetheart," she overheard Gage croon to Honey's momma.

Jess rounded the stall's corner to see him stroking the mare's mane. Gage seemed so gentle and kind. Responsible. Hardworking. Exactly the kind of hand she'd want. So why, *why* couldn't she take a gamble on letting him stay? So what if he took off? It wouldn't be the end of the world. He would just be a hired hand. She would find another.

"This little fella's looking better," Gage said, turning his attention to the colt. "Doc called my cell while you were refereeing the girls. Gave me a list of warning signs to watch for, but he looks good."

"How long have you known Doc?"

"Long as I can remember," he said, coming out of the stall for a handful of oats he fed the mare. "When my parents lived here, I guess they were friends with Doc and his wife. Over the years, they kept in touch."

"That's nice," Jess said, stroking Honey. "My parents have a few couples they've known forever. Every so often, they get together. Meet up for fun weekends in Dallas or Kansas City." He grabbed a pitchfork, and scooped manure into a wheelbarrow. "You look like you've done that before. Been around horses much?"

"All my life." After spreading fresh straw on the floor, he moved on to the next stall. "Well, all of my life, that is, save for recently."

"Right. I remember you saying you live in Dallas. But does your family still have a ranch?" She grabbed a second pitchfork so she could help.

"Yep."

"In Texas?" Jess probed.

"Uh-huh."

"So that's where you learned to work with horses?"

"Yep."

They both moved on to other stalls.

"How come you're not with them for Christmas? Your family?" Despite the barn's chill, beneath her heavy coat and sweater she was already working up a sweat.

"Long story."

"Thanks to the weather, looks like we'll be together a while."

"Ha-ha." He jabbed his pitchfork in the wheelbarrow's rapidly growing manure pile.

When Gage made no further conversational attempts, Jess prompted, "Well? Christmas? Your family?"

"Truth is, if it's all right by you, I'd rather not talk about it."

"Fair enough." She jabbed her fork alongside his. Lord knew, she had plenty of her own issues she'd rather not discuss. Still... Who voluntarily left their loved ones this time of year? "But why aren't you still work-ing for them?"

He snorted. "I'm all grown-up. Got a place of my own."

"Then why aren't you working your own land?"

With a fifty-pound feed sack over his shoulder, he sighed. "Am I on trial here?"

"Of course not. I'm just curious, that's all." Who wouldn't be? The guy was smart, strong. Admittedly had his own place to be working. His being here didn't add up.

But if Gage came along with Doc's endorsement, that guaranteed he was good people. Neither Doc, nor her parents, would ever put her and the girls in jeopardy. Meaning, Jess's best guess as to what Gage didn't want to talk about was some sort of family problem. Not es-pecially uncommon, but it must've been something pretty serious for him to not even want to be with them over the holidays.

He eyed her a good long while, as if he knew she was adding up what little she knew about him. Would he be upset with her for wanting to pry? Would he even care? After all, just as soon as the weather cleared, he'd be on his way. Back to Texas. Back to whatever troubles had driven him to Mercy. Which was a good thing. The best. She had enough troubles of her own.

"I'm not some criminal on the run if that's what you're thinking. And my place—it's a high-rise condo. Assuming you were wondering why I'm not working my own spread."

"No, no," she assured. "I wasn't wondering any-thing. Everyone's entitled to his or her privacy."

"I understand it probably sounds crazy for me to be

working your land when I could be working for my family, right?"

She nodded. "I've got my daughters to consider. I can't have them exposed to—"

"Look," he said, dropping the feed sack to his feet. "I've been through something I can't even begin to…" Through the open vee of his blue flannel shirt, Jess watched Gage's throat convulse. Sweat dampened his forehead and upper lip. His brown eyes welled, and then he looked away, shoulders slumped. "I can't talk about it, all right? But I promise you, Jess, I'm a good man. I have nothing but the best intentions toward you and your girls. If you don't believe me, ask—"

"I—I believe you." And she did. Because of Doc and her parents, but mostly because of the sincerity in his eyes. The raw pain in his expression. In his own time he'd open up. Assuming he even stayed that long. Which, of course, he wouldn't. But if things had been different, if he were staying, she would listen. The past year had made Jess an expert in tough times, whatever Gage's may be. Because it was Christmas Eve, her gift would be letting him keep those secrets of his.

Behind them, one of the dozen horses softly whinnied.

"Someone's hungry," she said.

"I'll tackle the feed if you check everyone's water."

"Deal."

Working in tandem, they quickly finished the chores. Forgetting about the haunted look in Gage's expression, Jess knew, would take much longer.

Chapter Four

"Go away." Lexie curved her arm over the picture she'd been drawing.

After helping to clean up lunch, Gage had debated whether to return to the bunkhouse or join Jess, who was wrapping presents in the living room. Still trying to decide, he'd wandered to the laundry room with a soiled dishrag only to stumble across Jess's oldest girl. She sat cross-legged on the linoleum floor, leaning against the running dryer. On her lap rested a clipboard. Beside her was a marker-filled basket.

Despite the room's tropical humidity and heat, Gage knelt beside the child. "Thought you didn't believe in Santa?"

"Who said this was for Santa?" she snapped. "I hate Santa. And *you*."

Atop a wintry scene of a snowman and a crudely drawn family of four was the heading: *Dear Santa, Please bring me my daddy for Chrismas.*

Throat tight, Gage wasn't sure what to say. "I'm, um, sorry you feel that way."

"I'm sorry you're still here."

Ouch. "Lex…?"

"Don't call me that. My name is Lex-*eeeeeeee.*"

"All right. Lexie…" He took a deep breath. "Santa? Real or fake?"

"Who are you?" she raged, ripping the drawing from its paper pad, crumpling it, then throwing it at him. "Why won't you just go away and mind your own—"

"Lexie!" Jess stood in the cramped room's threshold. "Go to your—" She needn't have wasted her breath, as the child had already bolted out the door.

Hand to his forehead, Gage said, "That could've gone better."

"What happened?" Jess asked.

The dryer buzzed.

She sighed.

"Let me get it," Gage said. "My sister used to pay me to do her laundry chores, so she could have more phone time. This makes me an expert in folding clothes."

"Thanks, but laundry's my job."

"I appreciate that, but seeing how I've got nothing better to do, how about just this once, letting laundry be *my* job?"

"Why?"

Grinning and shaking his head, Gage asked, "Woman, anyone ever tell you you're about as obstinate as your daughter?"

"All the time, which doesn't change the fact that you're a guest in my home."

"Then I should get to do pretty much whatever I want, right?"

"Well…" She nibbled her lower lip.

"Great decision." Gently nudging her aside, ignoring the hot rush of awareness caused by brushing his shoulder against hers, he tugged open the dryer and pulled out a warm blue towel to fold.

In the meantime, Jess had knelt to pick up her daughter's crumpled artwork. Smoothing it out atop the washer, upon seeing the heading, she covered her mouth with her hands. Her words low enough that she could've been talking to herself, Jess mumbled, "What am I going to do with her?"

"You asking me?" Gage asked, reaching for another towel—this one pink.

"No. I can handle my daughter all on my own."

"No offense, but from the outside, looking in, whatever methods you've been using to *handle* Lex don't seem to be working."

"First," Jess said, reaching around him and into the dryer for a pint-size white T-shirt, "I barely even know you, so why would I want your opinion? Second, seeing how I'm assuming you don't have kids, what do you know about picking up the pieces of a little girl's life after her father has died? Third—"

"I get it," Gage said, throwing a shirt onto the growing pile atop the dryer. "All you had to say is butt out, and—"

"Mommy?" Gage glanced down from the pair of yellow footy pajamas he'd been folding to see Ashley standing at the door. "Lex broke Tom." She held a T-rex body in one hand and the head in her other. "Can you fix it?"

"I don't know, sweetie. I can try." As if counting to ten in her head, Jess clamped her hand to her forehead. "Usually, plastic like that is tough to glue."

"Mind if I take a look?" Gage asked, putting the pj's on the laundry pile before kneeling before the girl.

"Sure," Ashley said, offering him the broken toy.

"While looking for the tire chains, I ran across some tools. Mind if I use the drill?" Surveying the damage, he added, "I'm thinking if I add a dowel to these pieces, then glue them, Tom might be saved."

"Can I help?" Ashley asked.

"If it's all right with your mom," Gage said.

Eyes wide and red-rimmed, the child looked to her mother. "Can I?"

Jess swallowed hard, then nodded. "Bundle up. The ice is still coming down pretty hard."

"I will." Ashley raced off for her coat, hat and mittens. "Come on, Mister Gage."

"Thanks," Jess said. "For whatever reason, she loves that dinosaur. It'd mean a lot to her if you could fix it."

"No problem." He turned to follow Ashley, when it occurred to him he hadn't finished folding. "Want me to tackle the rest of the load before I go?"

As she shook her head wearing a faint smile, her mood was indecipherable. Full lips slightly parted, eyes glistening. Sad? Angry? Defeated? However ludicrous it may sound, on an instinctual level, he craved knowing what Jess felt—about everything.

Most especially, him.

"HEY," JESS SAID, perching on the foot of Lexie's twin bed. The room's theme was Barbie, and everything from the walls to the curtains to the bedspread was pink. Just like Lexie used to be in spirit before Dwayne's passing. Pink and bubbly and full of life. Now, she reminded Jess more of some morose Goth teen. "Wanna talk?"

"No." The girl was curled up in bed, hugging the giant panda her grandparents had given her last year for her birthday. She and the panda were nestled beneath a fuzzy pink blanket, covering all but their heads.

"Great. I'm so glad you've decided to open up."

Tightening her hold on the bear, Lexie gave her mom the quintessential angry-kid look. The one that said *I'll gladly trade my every earthly possession for you to vanish from my room.*

"I found this…." From her back pocket, Jess withdrew Lexie's drawing for Santa.

"I didn't make it."

"Sweetie…" Jess sighed. "Don't make this worse by lying."

"All right," she said, hiding her face against the bear's belly. "I made the stupid drawing. But I don't believe in Santa."

"No one said you had to."

"I don't." Lexie pulled the covers over her head.

"It is an awfully nice drawing, though. Even though it makes me sad."

"Why?" Eyes big and wet, Jess's little girl peeked out from under the blanket.

"Because I know that even Santa can't bring back your dad. No matter how bad you wish he could."

"I know. I'm not stupid." She resorted back to hiding.

"Did I say you were?" Jess rubbed the girl's back. "Pumpkin… I'm worried about you. You seem so angry. And not just with Gage, but me and your sister. Grandma and Grandpa. You didn't used to be this way and I—"

"Why won't you leave me alone?" Bursting out from under the covers, letting her bear fall to the floor, Lexie ran out of her room and into the bathroom across the hall.

Jess flinched when the girl slammed the door.

She eased her fingers into the hair at her temples, almost as if by tugging at it, she might withdraw an answer as to how to help her daughter. It'd been over a year since Dwayne's accident. During a torrential downpour, he'd been shoring up the dam of an embankment pond when it had broken, flipping the backhoe and pinning him beneath. Jess's mom had always told her time healed all wounds, but in Lexie's case, time hadn't helped.

Easing up from the bed, she followed her daughter's trail, knocking on the bathroom door. "Please, Lex, talk to me. Cry. Scream. Yell. Whatever you need to do to let out your pain."

After a few moments, the door opened and out walked Lexie, seemingly calm and composed. "Are we still making Christmas cookies?"

"YOU'RE SMART," Ashley said in the workshop that was tucked into a corner of the barn. A small electric heater pumped out just enough warmth to remind Gage how frigid it really was. While he changed the drill bit to one small enough to match the dowel he'd be using to join Tom's broken halves, the girl watched with rapt interest. "How'd you learn to do all this?"

"My dad. He's a good guy. *Very* smart—about lots of things."

"Is he dead? My daddy is."

Ouch. Ashley's matter-of-fact statement hit hard. On the one hand, it was great that she could so frankly discuss her dad's demise. On the other, what kind of seven-year-old talked about death as if it were as commonplace as a cloudy day?

"My dad's alive," he said. "B-but my sister isn't."

"Sometimes I wish my sister was dead." She climbed up onto a wooden stool, kicking her booted feet. "Sometimes I even wish she'd gone to Heaven instead of Daddy."

Double ouch. For a place where he'd intended to come to forget about death, why did the topic seem to pervade every conversation? "You don't really mean that?" he asked with a sideways glance in her direction. "About your sister?"

"Sometimes I do. Like when she broke Tom. She was just being mean. I think she blames me for Daddy dying, but I wasn't even there when his accident happened."

"What was his accident?" Gage felt bad pumping a kid for information on such an adult topic, but sick curiosity got the better of him.

"All I know is," she said, still kicking her feet, "he was doing something with his tractor, and got hurt bad. Mommy doesn't like talking about it. Gramma and Grandpa don't, either." While Gage fit the dowel into the dinosaur's head and body, adding glue to both parts before pushing them together, the girl silently watched on. "Mister Gage?"

"Yeah?"

"Do you think my family wants to forget Daddy? Because it's almost Christmas, and I don't think that's very nice."

"I don't think that at all," he said, handing her the fixed toy. "In fact, what I think is going on is that they all love your dad so much, that it hurts them to talk about him. I think deep inside—you know, in their hearts—they talk about him all the time. But it's quiet so you can't hear."

Scrunching up her nose and cocking her head, she asked, "Kind of like when you pray?"

"Exactly," he said with a tweak to her adorable button nose, wishing for so much as an ounce of her wisdom.

THOUGH ALREADY stuffed from a simple meal of beef stew and corn bread, Gage helped himself to another Santa-shaped, iced sugar cookie.

"Jess, girls," he said, nodding to all. "Thank you. This was good."

Yet again, he'd been starving. Prior to dinner, while Jess had hung out with Ashley doing the whole baking thing, he'd been in the barn, tending to Honey and the rest of the horses. Hard work was proving to be effective medicine.

"We're the *best* cookie makers," Ashley said, making no attempt to be humble.

"I agree." Gage reached for a colorfully iced Christmas tree and chomped off the top.

Meanwhile, Ashley took two angels. One for herself, and the other for Taffy, who'd been lying patiently at her feet, occasionally glancing up at the girl with doe-eyed longing.

"Did you know you've had five of those?" Lexie scowled in Gage's direction.

"Sorry," he said, pausing midbite, not sure what to make of the kid's hostility. "Were you saving the trees?"

"Yes. But now you ruined everything, so go ahead and eat them."

"Lexie," Jess warned, "please apologize to our guest."

Her apology consisted of sticking out her tongue, then making a mad dash for the stairs.

"She needs help," Ashley said, shaking her head.

From the mouths of babes...

Not sure what else to do, Gage cleared his throat.

"I should go talk to her," Jess said, "but, I'm beginning to think all the talk in the world isn't going to do any good."

"I think she needs a spankin'," said their resident psychiatrist before snatching a frosted stocking.

"Ashley, kindly stay out of it."

"Maybe the kid's right," Gage suggested. "I've heard of tough love being great for some kids. You know, like a boot camp regime."

Jess shot him an incredulous look. "Are you honestly suggesting I send my nine-year-old daughter to boot camp?"

"No. But maybe you could simulate something like it at home. You know, help her get to the bottom of whatever's eating her with hard work." Not that he was an expert, but it'd already been beneficial to him.

"Ashley," Jess said as she reached to the table's center for the cookie platter, "please take these into the TV room, and pop in a Christmas movie. I'll be right there."

"But how come I can't stay *here?*"

Lips momentarily pressed tight, Jess said, "Because I told you to go to the TV room and watch a movie."

"Oh." Ashley glanced from Gage to her mom, then, clutching Tom with one hand and the cookie tray with her other, scampered off.

Taffy followed along, toenails clacking.

"Look," Jess said once her youngest was out of earshot, "I wholeheartedly appreciate your advice, but I can handle my own daughter."

"With all due respect," Gage said, fingers tented on the table, "your kid seems to be in trouble. Unless you want a certified nutcase on your hands by the time she's a teen, you may want to confront the situation head-on now."

Eyes narrowed, mouth pinched, Jess looked ready to leap across the table and wring his neck. "What don't you understand about the fact that I handle my own affairs? The last thing I need is advice from an outsider."

He snorted. "Lady, judging by your spit viper of a kid, you don't just need my advice, but an army full."

"Okay, Mr. Child-rearing Expert, if Lexie were yours, how would you handle the situation?"

"First off, I wouldn't treat her with kid gloves. You sending her to her room all the time has gotten to be a treat. You're rewarding her antisocial behavior by telling her to go ahead and be even more antisocial. Second—"

When silent tears streamed down Jess's cheeks, Gage knew he'd gone too far.

"Aw, hell…" Pushing up from the table, he went to her, awkwardly coming up behind her for a hug. "I'm sorry. You're right. This is none of my business, and in a few days I'll be leaving, and then—"

"No," she said with a sniffle, "as much as it hurts to admit, you're right. I can't let Lexie go on this way. You're not the first person she's had it in for. And unless I do something drastic, you won't be the last. Mom and Dad and I—even Doc and Martha—have discussed what to do, but we're all too close. We all remember what Lexie was like with her dad, and it's just too painful to come down hard on her for wanting him back."

"I know the feeling," Gage said, returning to his seat all the way across the table from Jess. Hugging her had felt good—too good. Especially since he'd been the one doing all the touching. Well, Jess had covered his hands with hers. And in that moment, for the briefest of seconds, he hadn't felt so alone.

Jess asked, "You've lost someone close?"

"Yeah, but back to Lexie—"

"Nope." Elbows on the table, Jess leaned forward. "You've tried this avoidance technique before, mister.

This time, it's not going to work. I've poured my heart out to you about Lexie. The least you can do is—"

"My sister. About three months ago—" His voice cracked.

"Sorry." Voice velvety and warm, she added, "That's all I need to know. Tell me more when you feel ready."

Right. Like twenty years from now Jess would still be in his life? He wasn't even sure if he'd see her again in twenty-four hours.

"Listen to us," she said with forced gaiety. "It's Christmas Eve, and we sound like some freakish clan of morose elves."

"Yeah," he said with a sad grin, "but at least we're good-lookin' morose elves."

"I'll toast to that," she said, raising her glass of milk to his.

For a split second, during shared smiles, Gage forgot everything and just enjoyed the moment. Actually *lived* in the moment. The feeling was intoxicating and he wanted more. Only experience had taught him happiness was a fleeting, migratory thing. One minute—one second—you basked in its glow, the next, reality reared its ugly head, informing you of the real score.

In the awkward silence, Gage cleared his throat. "If you think it would make life easier for you—" translation: temporarily nullify Lexie until after Christmas "—want me to head back to the bunkhouse and stay there 'til the weather clears?"

Chapter Five

"What?" Gage's question caught her so off guard, Jess actually shook her head. "I thought we were having a nice time. Why would you want to hole up in that dreary little bunkhouse?"

"Dreary?" Eyebrows raised, he said, "Your bunkhouse is a full-on guest lodge compared to some of the places I've stayed."

Of course. She'd forgotten all of the hard work her mother and Martha had put into the place while she'd been off checking fences. Okay, so if her objection to his bailing on her had nothing to do with his living quarters, then what? She understood that he thought Lexie might be more of her normal self with him gone. What Jess didn't get was why, at the thought of him leaving, her stomach knotted and the child in her who still believed in Christmas magic felt as if she'd been Scrooged.

"Jess?"

"Look," she managed to say after a deep, calming breath, "I know this may sound crazy, but I want you to stay. I-it's been a while since I've had a friend, and well… Not that I'm implying we are already friends, just that—"

"Hey," he said, sliding his hand across the table,

fingers touching the tips of hers—*electrifying* the tips of hers.

Instinctively, she flinched. Drew her still-tingling hand to her lap.

"Sorry," he said, retreating to his own personal space.

"No." She gulped. "I'm sorry. You were only trying to comfort me, and here I am acting like some—"

"Enough with the apologies, Jess. What you're acting like is a woman who was… Hell, for lack of a better term, *felt up,* by some strange man. I'm the one who should be apologizing."

"Stop." Forcing air into failing lungs, Jess summoned the courage to move her hand to his. Only she didn't just touch him, but gripped him. Held on for dear life. "Truthfully, I backed away, because your fingers against mine felt…"

"Good?"

The knot at the back of her throat only allowed her to nod before taking back her hand.

"Me, too. But you have to know I didn't mean anything by it, okay? I mean, during your whole *friend* speech, I was thinking, yeah, that's why I've been so relaxed around you and Ashley—no offense to Lex."

Jess grinned.

"It's been a while since I've met anyone new. Especially anyone I cared enough about to share a meal with or… You know—conversation."

"Yes. I do know. But you and I becoming fast friends doesn't even seem possible. I don't even know what you do. For a living, that is. Are you a professional ranch hand?"

Snorting, he said, "My chronically aching back wishes. I'm on the pro bull-rider circuit. During deep winter and spring storms, I'd swear I've got more broke bones in this old body than not."

"You're hardly old," she said.

"True, but with me, that saying about being as old as you feel has never been more true."

"In high school," Jess admitted, "I used to barrel race. I was pretty good, too."

"Why'd you stop?"

"Boys," she blurted, before ducking her heated gaze. "God never did make a prettier sight than a cowboy's behind." Hand to her mouth, she laughed. "Did I actually just say that?"

"Yes, ma'am," Gage said with a chuckle, "I believe you did."

"Maybe this isn't plain old milk," she said, eyeing her glass, "but spiked eggnog?"

"If it makes you feel better, I've got a thing for rodeo queens." He winked. "Some of their behinds are also mighty fine."

"Mmm…one of these days I'll have to show you my crown," she teased.

"You were royalty, huh?" He raised his eyebrows.

"You don't have to look so shocked. At sixteen, I was Miss Rodeo Mercy." She happened to glance down at her hands, work-worn and scarred. Chapped from wind and cold. No wonder Gage had looked so surprised. Aside from a lack of barbed-wire scars, her facial complexion wasn't much better. What would any man ever see in her again? Not that she was looking for male companionship, but on the off-chance she ever did get a harebrained notion to date, then—

"Got pictures?"

"Of what? My reign?"

"Duh." His grin made her stomach somersault. Lord, but the man was handsome.

"I suppose I've got snapshots around here some-where. I'd have to—"

"Mommy," Ashley asked, "when are we going to sing?"

"I'm sorry, sweetie." She drew her child into a hug. She'd been so wrapped up in shameless flirting, she'd forgotten about their caroling tradition. Usually, they gathered around the fire at her parents' place, or with Dwayne's folks. Not that it was an excuse, but without family, it didn't even feel like Christmas.

Really? Then how come sharing laughter with Gage had seemed like a wonderful gift? Only not the kind that comes with pretty wrappings, but the priceless variety stemming from human warmth and kindness. The true spirit of the holidays that all too often seemed forgotten.

"Where's your sister?" Jess asked. "And did you already get out the songbooks?" For Lexie's first Christmas, Jess's mom had made elaborate, hand-bound caroling books with lyrics to help the family through those awkward spots where everyone stands around and hums.

"I don't know, and yep."

"Could you please find Lexie for me?"

Ashley made a face.

"Please? Gage and I will make hot cocoa and meet you and Taffy in front of the fire."

When Ashley had left, Gage said, "Thought I was heading back to the bunkhouse?"

"Thanks for the suggestion," Jess said, taking milk from the fridge, "but with Lexie so down in the dumps, I'm thinking Ashley and I could use a friend."

"SIIIIII-LENT NIGHT… Hooooo-ly night…"

All three of the girls had high, crystalline voices that warmed the frigid night. Outside, ice still hammered the tin roof and occasional wind bursts shuddered the walls. Inside, with flames dancing in the fieldstone hearth and candles and the glowing multicolored bulbs on the Christmas tree lighting the room, they might've been in another era. Save for the electrically lit tree, they could have been early Oklahoma settlers, celebrating their first holiday in a new sod house. Judging by the place's run-down exterior, it was probably about as well-insulated as a sod shanty.

He'd always loved the scent of pine, and the fresh-cut tree smelled amazing.

Though Gage occasionally joined in, he'd never been big on singing, preferring to listen, letting the music soothe parts of him Marnie's passing had left emotionally battered.

Jess and her girls sat in a half circle on a thick rag rug in front of the fire, Taffy sleeping in the center. Even Lexie seemed to enjoy the tradition, going so far as to flash an occasional smile.

Gage wished he could say he was having a good time, but it was really more of a confusing time. Torn, a part of him missed his family. Without Marnie, this would be a wretched holiday season. Gage knew he should be there for his mom and dad, but couldn't. The guilt was too raw. Memories of her death too vivid.

"Feliz Navidad… Feliz Navidad…" Lexie and Jess launched into the Spanish favorite.

"I don't like this one," Ashley whispered, "but do you think we did a good job on the last one?" She'd come to stand next to where he'd settled on the far edge of the sofa, gazing expectantly up at him. Poor kid.

Must be tough being so hungry for a male role model that she'd turned to a screwup like him.

"You did great," he said past the knot in his throat. If only he could say the same about himself. If only he'd fought harder. Had enough sense to know Marnie was in trouble before it'd been too late.

"Are you crying?" Ashley asked.

Turning his head, Gage wiped his eyes with the heels of his hands. "No," he assured the girl. "Just had dust in my eye."

"Oh." Her wide stare said she didn't believe him.

While Lexie and Jess kept singing, Ashley seized his heart by sticking her small hand in his. "You can't cry on Christmas, Mister Gage. Santa wants you to be happy."

"I'm good. Promise."

"Okay... But if you feel sad, you can talk to me. Lots of times, I feel sad about Daddy, but I go get a hug from Mommy or one of my grammas and then I feel better. If you want, I'm sure Mommy could hug you, too."

The suggestion, coming from such an unexpected source, was at once preposterous, yet tempting. At the moment, he'd like nothing better than a hug, but he didn't want to get any closer to Jess. He simply couldn't emotionally afford it. Not only had she admitted she didn't want him here past the storm, but he also wasn't worthy of being a friend. For his having been blind to Marnie's every trouble sign, he didn't deserve any woman's affection. Be it friendship or something more.

"Mister Gage?" Ashley prompted, squeezing his index finger. "Want me to ask Mommy about your hug?"

"No, thank you. I promise, I feel great. Just had something in my eye. Maybe a bug. Or a dinosaur egg."

"Whoa. No wonder you were crying. That *would* hurt."

"What would hurt?" Jess asked, her arm companionably around Lexie's slim shoulders.

"Mister Gage has a dinosaur egg in his eye. That's why he was crying. But he's better now."

Jess's concerned glance told him she wasn't buying the dino story. Out of view of the girls, she mouthed, *You okay?*

He nodded.

She frowned.

"Come on, Mom," Lexie urged. "Let's do, 'Deck the Halls'."

"How about joining us?" Jess asked him. Her eyes said, *It might make you feel better.*

"One song," he said, "but that's my official limit."

"Fair enough."

One song led to about seven badly bungled carols that had Gage laughing so hard his sides hurt.

"See?" Jess said when the girls headed for the kitchen for more cocoa. "You're a much better singer than you let on."

"Either that, or you're tone-deaf."

"Hey!" She elbowed his ribs. "I happen to be a very good judge of talent."

"How so?"

"Well…" Her grin was mesmerizing—not a good thing, considering he'd already determined that he had no business being attracted to her. "Truthfully, I've never been like an official talent scout or anything, but whenever a new song comes on the radio, I predict with uncanny accuracy whether or not it'll be a hit."

"Oh, you do? And I'm star material?"

"Definitely." The twinkle in her eyes belied her words.

"Mommy?" Ashley asked, upper lip white from the melting minimarshmallows heaped in her cocoa. "Can we open one present tonight? You let us last year."

"Grandma and Grandpa Cummings left a couple of packages in the front closet that might have your names on them."

"Cool!" Ashley ran for the gifts.

Lexie took off at a more dignified pace.

"I wish I had something for the girls," Gage said.

Jess waved off his suggestion. "Thanks, but trust me, between two sets of grandparents and Doc and Martha, both will have a merry enough Christmas."

"How about you?"

She laughed. "I'm too old to get excited about presents."

"That's sad," he said, wishing he were within walking distance of a mall so that he could purchase her something big and shiny and worthy of Christmas-morning awe. If she were his, he'd make it a personal challenge to show her just how much fun ripping into brightly wrapped surprises could be.

"How is it sad? I had fun as a kid—even as a newly-wed, but since… Anyway, I learned that it's time to grow up. I have to be strong for my girls and make sure their needs and wants are met before even contemplating mine."

"When's the last time you did something nice for yourself?"

"Like what? Do you suggest I abandon my daily chores to lounge at some fancy spa?" She made a show of fluffing her already mussed hair. She'd no doubt meant to look silly, but all she'd ended up doing was looking prettier than ever. More wholesome and good and determined to do right by her daughters.

"When's the last time you've soaked in a steaming bubble bath?"

She rolled her eyes. "I don't have time. But I suppose you do?"

Now he was rolling his eyes, while the girls danced back in, wearing huge reindeer slippers and chewing equally huge wads of pink gum.

"Look, Mommy," Ashley said, wagging her left foot, "what we got."

"I see. Now you can help Santa make his rounds."

Lexie scoffed at the suggestion.

"Santa's *real,* Lexie." Ashley stood scowling, hands on her hips. "You'll know he's real when you get *nothing* in the morning."

"That's enough," Jess scolded. "Both of you go on upstairs and get ready for bed. And just because it's Christmas Eve doesn't mean you don't have to brush your teeth."

"Aw, man…" As usual, Lexie wasn't happy.

"Go on," Jess said, standing in front of the sofa while hollering up the stairs, "I'll be there in a sec to tuck you in."

"Guess I should be going, too." Gage rose, dreading leaving the toasty living room to reenter the world of ice. Even more, he dreaded leaving Jess. Her presence calmed him in a way he didn't begin to understand. Truth be known, he didn't want to understand. But he didn't want to be sucked deeper into Jess Cummings's spell. And she did have a spell. An air of need all tangled up with strength. He wanted to lighten her workload. Her emotional load. Her every problem so as to make way for more of her luminous smiles.

"Thanks for hanging out with us." She lifted her arms as if she wanted to hug him, but then lowered them, cramming her hands into her jeans pockets. "It was probably a drag, but—"

"I had a nice time. Thank you for including me in such an intimate family occasion."

"You're welcome…." She held her full lips partially open, as if she had more to say, but didn't—or couldn't express it.

"Mommy!" Ashley bellowed. "We're done!"

"Guess I'm being summoned." Jess flashed a weary grimace. "Sure you'll be all right?"

"Yep. Go ahead and tend to your girls. I'll stop by the barn to see how Honey and the rest of the gang are faring. Make sure their water hasn't frozen over."

"The horses." A cloud fell on her soft features. "I check them every night. How could I have forgotten?"

"Don't sweat it. Everyone's entitled to a night off now and then."

"You know as well as I do that when it comes to animals, there's no such thing as *off* time. They're like my children. I'm responsible for them, and I need—"

Planting work-roughened hands on either side of her face, he kissed her quiet, not giving a damn whether it was appropriate or not. In the heat of the moment, all he could think of was soothing her, calming her, bringing back her smile. "What you need is to hush."

Expression dazed, she raised trembling hands to her lips.

"That's better." Softly cupping her shoulders, hoping she wasn't on the verge of spitting fire, he added, "Now, go see after your munchkins and let me handle everything else."

"I can't—" Her shining eyes were damp, but not so much as a single tear fell.

"Dammit, woman," he said with a barely perceptible

squeeze, "am I going to have to carry you up those stairs?"

"Mommy!" Ashley was at it again, shaking the rafters with the decibels of her yell.

"I—I don't know what to say." Gage couldn't begin to decipher the emotions flickering across Jess's face.

"How about 'good night'?"

"Moooooom-eeeeee!"

Not wanting the tongue-lashing he feared Jess was on the verge of unleashing, Gage aimed for the front door. He shrugged on his coat, boots and hat, then escaped into the night.

FINGERS TREMBLING, Jess raised them to her mouth. What had Gage been thinking? Well, obviously, he hadn't been. Thinking, that is.

Her tingling lips were traitorous and infuriating and—

"Mooooooooom-eeee!"

"B-be right there!" Even though she'd shouted her reply, Jess could hardly hear her voice over her pounding heart. What had she done? Not that she'd been the one initiating the kiss, but the fact that she hadn't shoved Gage away and run screaming had to be significant, right?

Legs numb, Jess somehow mounted the stairs and went through the motions of getting her girls in bed.

"Mom?" Lexie asked after she'd been tucked in.

"Yes, ma'am?" Jess perched on the edge of her daughter's bed. The room's air was chilly, but just right for snuggling under a down comforter. The only light came from a small crystal lamp that had been Jess's when she was a little girl.

"Is that Gage guy going to be gone in the morning?"

I wish. "No." Smoothing her daughter's hair back from her forehead and tucking it behind her ears, she said, "In fact, he'll be here for breakfast and opening our presents and I'd appreciate you being polite." Why? When Jess wasn't sure she even wanted to see him again, let alone share the most intimate of holiday gatherings with him.

"But I don't like him. He's mean."

"No, sweetie, he's not." In fact, as shocking as his kiss had been, his conversation had been that comfortable. Like slipping into her favorite flannel pj's after a long day's work. Something about him drew her in.

Unexplainable, inexplicable, but there all the same.

"I'm not going to talk to him," Lexie said.

"That's fine. In fact, seeing how everything leaving your mouth lately has been rude, maybe it'd be best if you were quiet."

"You're mean!" Rolling over, Lexie drew the covers over her head. "And I *am* going to talk. A lot!"

"Well…" Not that she'd admit it to Lexie, but nothing would make Jess happier than for her daughter to revert back to the chatterbox she used to be. "I hate to hear that, but if that's the way you feel, I don't suppose I can stop you." Any more than Jess could squelch the seed of anticipation rising at the thought of seeing Gage again. Talking with him.

Laughing with him.

Kissing him?

Mortification flamed her cheeks.

Chapter Six

In the barn's back room, Gage trailed his hands along Jess's husband's dusty tools. Poor guy. He'd had it all. A great woman. Great kids. Nice stretch of land. Didn't come much better than that.

There'd been a day when Gage had wanted nothing more for himself, but then Marnie had been killed and in that instant, everything changed. Whereas before, Gage had lived his life in the moment. In the eight seconds of a bull ride, the ten seconds it took to swig a beer after a ride, the thirty-six hundred seconds worth of loving a rodeo queen decked out in nothing but red boots and her crown. After his sister's death, days— seconds—seemed to have grown inexplicably long. Unbearable to count, let alone live.

A horse neighed, returning Gage to the present. To the tasks he'd stayed in the barn to do. Dwayne's tools would make for light work.

Using wood chisels and sandpaper and a lathe, he fashioned simple gifts for the family he'd spend Christmas morning with. A year earlier, the thought of spending the holiday with anyone other than his own family would have been unthinkable. Yet now, solace came with the knowledge that he wouldn't have to face his parents' accusing eyes. With their words, they told him what happened wasn't his fault. But their eyes…

Over and over he worked the wood, losing himself in smoothing rough planes.

The longer he worked, the more frigid the air grew. The larger the cloud of his breath. Even when his fingertips grew numb from cold, he kept on long into the night. Until his muscles ached and his eyes stung. Until the emotional pain faded to a manageable level. Until he fell onto his soft bed and drifted into dreamless sleep.

"PSST… ARE YOU DEAD?"

Gage cracked open his right eye, finding himself face-to-face with Jess's smallest munchkin.

"Well?" Ashley asked.

Fully awake, though not entirely happy about it, Gage shifted up in the bed. "Not only am I alive, but tired. What brings you to my neck of the woods at this ungodly early hour?"

"Huh?" The girl scrunched her nose. "We're not in the woods, and I don't know what else you said, but Mommy said I should see if you're up so that we can eat pancakes or else she won't let us open presents."

"Oh…" With his left hand, he rubbed weary eyes.

"Come on, hurry!" Tugging his arm, the kid showed a surprising amount of strength. Gage admired that—her spunk.

"Tell you what," he said, wishing he wore more than boxers. "Scamper on back to the house, and I'll be right there."

"Yeah," Ashley argued, "but if you don't come *now*, it'll be *forever* before we get presents."

"Let's make a deal…." Gage tugged the covers she'd

pulled down back up to his chest. "You get on back to the house, and I'll give you a present from me while we eat."

"You got something for me?"

He nodded.

"Where?" Her eyes widened. "You couldn't even get to the store."

"True enough." He winked. "Which is why you'd better be good. This present is from the big man himself."

The girl's eyes grew wide. "You mean...Santa?"

Gage solemnly nodded.

"Bye!"

As the kid dashed for the door, Gage laughed. On the off chance he ever became a father, he'd have to remember to never underestimate the power of good old Saint Nick.

"YOU'RE LATE." As Gage entered the back door, slamming it shut against howling wind, Lexie shot him her most dirty look.

"Hush!" Jess cringed at her daughter's already less-than-cordial behavior. So much for her vow not to speak.

"Merry Christmas." Though Gage still had some explaining to do in regard to that kiss, Jess greeted him with a warm smile. Could that skip in her pulse mean she was actually glad to see him?

"Sorry, if I've held y'all up." Gage shrugged off his snow-dusted cowboy hat and coat. He held on to the hat while slinging the coat over the back of the nearest kitchen table chair.

Taffy licked melting snow from the floor.

"That's not where your jacket goes," Lexie was all too happy to point out.

Gage picked it back up and tossed it to her. "Mind putting it where it should be?"

The girl's openmouthed expression was priceless. Glancing to Jess, she asked, "Do I have to?"

"If you'd like presents instead of a bag of switches."

Lexie sighed, but took the coat toward the entry hall, where Jess presumed poor Gage's outerwear would be dumped on the closet floor.

"Sorry about that," Jess said, trying not to notice how the cold had ruddied Gage's whisker-stubbled cheeks. Or how the brown in his eyes reminded her of milk chocolate. Sweet and loaded with sin. Handsome didn't begin to describe him. Which was why she looked away, focusing on the fragrant cinnamon rolls needing to be taken from the oven.

"No problem," he said.

"Actually, it is very much a problem, and we both know it. But for today, at least, we'll pretend all is well in the world."

"Deal." His slow grin made something in her stomach somersault.

While a peek through fogged windows showed the storm raged on outside, and now blanketed their icy world in snow, the kitchen was toasty. Maybe even a touch too warm, since Gage had appeared. Jess fought the urge to change from her white sweatshirt and red flannel pj bottoms into shorts and a T-shirt.

"Mommy?" Ashley asked, out of breath from running into the room.

"Yes, hon?"

"Is Lexie supposed to be peeking at her presents?"

"You mean like actually unwrapping them?" With her behind, Jess bumped closed the oven door.

"Nice technique," Gage said with a sassy wink.

Ignoring him, along with the flash of awareness stemming from him standing just a few feet away, Jess said to her youngest, "Unless she's tearing off paper, leave her alone."

"Okay," Ashley said, slumping into a chair, "but if she opens all my presents, I'm gonna be really mad."

"Duly noted." With the spatula, Jess scooped cinnamon rolls from a cookie sheet to a Christmas platter, which she then set in the center of the table. Already prepared and still warm under foil were bacon and pancakes with softened butter and hot syrup.

"This is quite a spread," Gage said with an appreciative whistle. "Need help?"

"No, thanks." Because truth be told, if he came much closer, Jess doubted she'd still have the sanity to cook. She'd thought herself free of the memory of his kiss, but she wasn't even close. And this was one case where she didn't think *trying* to forget counted.

"I'll help, Mom." Lexie appeared at her side, her face wreathed in a rare smile.

"Thanks, sweetie." Jess handed her daughter the bacon, directing her to set it on the table. It didn't take a rocket scientist to figure out Lexie's sudden altruistic streak wasn't from the goodness of her heart, but rather a desire to prove herself better than Gage. But again, in the spirit of the day, Jess chose to let it go.

"You're welcome." Lexie aimed her thousand-watt smile at Gage.

Thankfully, the rest of the meal passed in a flurry of passing this and that. Ashley was so antsy to see what Santa brought, she nearly fell out of her chair. Lucky for her, Taffy was on hand, gobbling what fell off her fork.

"Mister Gage?" Ashley asked, impatience lending a whine to her tone.

"Uh-huh?" His mouth was full of pancakes. Was it wrong for Jess to take pride in the fact that he enjoyed her cooking?

"Back at the bunkhouse, you said if I left you alone, you'd let me have a present during breakfast."

"That, I did." He helped himself to more bacon.

"Well?" Her fidgeting had reached a fevered, Christmas-morning pitch.

"Tell you what," he said, bacon to his lips. "I'm thinking if you head into the laundry room, Santa might've hid something for you by the back door."

"Really?" Ashley was already out of her chair and running in that direction.

Lexie, meanwhile, used her butter knife to swirl patterns in her syrup.

"I don't see it!" Even with a muffled voice, Ashley's panic rang out.

"Right alongside the washer." Was it wrong that when Gage shot a wink in Jess's direction, her pulse was as fidgety as her youngest girl?

"You didn't have to bring her anything," Jess said. But how wonderful and kind that he had.

"I know. But it's Christmas, and seeing how you've gifted me with a warm place to stay and plenty of good eats, I figured bringing a smile to your girls' faces was the least I could do."

"You said *girls*." Lexie shot him a squinty-eyed glare. "Does that mean you got me something, too?"

"Lexie!" Jess fought the urge to hide under the table.

"It's okay," Gage said with an indulgent chuckle. "As a matter of fact, Santa left something for you, too."

"Santa's not real," Lexie reminded him.

"That may well be," Gage said with one of his trade-mark slow grins, "but the present he left you looks real enough to me. Check on top of the dryer."

"Gage," Jess said under her breath, "you didn't have to—"

"Rrrrrrr!" Ashley leaped out from behind her mom's chair, brandishing a new dinosaur.

Taffy barked.

"It's okay," Ashley said to the dog, rubbing him between his ears. "This is a baby dinosaur. He won't eat you—or you, Mommy." She grinned. "I just wanted to scare you."

"That's a relief." Jess clutched her chest, but not so much out of fear, but gratitude. The dinosaur, carved from pine, was exquisite. How Gage had accomplished something so adorable in so short a time was inconceivable. That he'd cared enough to create the gift for her little girl was—

"Mister Gage…" Lexie entered the room, chin hugging her chest. Cradled in her arms was a doll-sized covered wagon. Eyes shining, she said, "I—I can't take this."

"Why?" Gage asked. "Santa told me that he made it especially for you."

"Ashley…" Turning to her sister, Lexie said, "Cover your ears."

Ashley held her hand over one ear and crammed the dinosaur's snout into her other.

Jess cringed.

"Now that she's not listening," Lexie said, her voice and expression solemn as she gently set the wagon on the table in front of Gage, "I know you made this and not Santa, because Santa isn't real."

Jess's eyes welled.

Gage cleared his throat.

Ashley was humming, twirling in a slow circle with the dino nose still in her ear.

"Yes, Lexie," Gage admitted, "I made you the wagon. And you're right, it wasn't Santa who wanted you to have it, but me. When you told me your dolls had to camp under the stars, I felt bad for them—and you."

"That's why I can't keep it," Lexie said. "Because I don't want you to feel bad for me. Me and my dolls are gonna be *fine* sleeping outside."

Whereas Jess's heart had felt lighter, she now worried for her daughter more than ever. What normal child gave away such a magical toy? As perfect as Ashley's dinosaur was, the Conestoga wagon was that much better—it was amazing, from the spoke wheels to the calico cover, no doubt, fabric borrowed from a bunkhouse pillowcase, and teeny seats just right for Barbie behinds. Dwayne had loved working with his hands, and only by using all of her husband's tools could Gage have made the toy so quickly.

"Can I open my ears?" Ashley asked with a big sigh.

"Yes," Jess said.

"May I please be excused?" Lexie asked.

"No." Standing, Jess said, "I'd like you and Ashley to please clear the table."

"But it's Christmas," Lexie complained.

"Yep," Jess told her daughter, "and while I'm checking the horses, you two can also load the dishwasher. When I get back, we'll open presents."

"Come on, Lex." Racing for the table, Ashley abandoned her new toy to load up with dirty dishes.

Not wanting to hear Lexie's grumbling—more importantly, needing alone time to relieve the knot in her throat—Jess left the kitchen for the front hall.

Unfortunately, Gage was hot on her heels, saying under his breath, "I, ah, don't mean to get in your business, but I've already fed and watered the horses."

Shoulders sagging, Jess sighed. "Great. Just great." Never had she thought she'd be disappointed by someone having done her chores.

"Sorry," Gage offered. "Thought I was doing you a favor—it being Christmas, and all."

"Y-you were. It's just that—" She shook her head, shoved her arms into her jacket, then opened the front door. Tears burned hot, then cold, as frigid air and wind slapped her face.

"Jess?" Grasping her upper arm, Gage tugged her back. His gaze was searching. Questioning. Confused. But no one could possibly be more mixed up than herself. "Stay inside. It's cold."

"I—I can't," she said, tears threatening to spill.

Outside, the white was blinding. The cold stole her breath. Snow fell in cottony clumps so thick she could hardly see the barn. Not that it would have mattered, considering how tears were now falling faster than the snow.

She'd left the house so abruptly, she'd forgotten to change from vinyl-soled house shoes to boots. Twenty feet into her trek, her toes turned numb.

"Jess!" Again, Gage chased after her. "Jeez, woman, you trying to catch your death of cold?"

Jess kept on trudging through the snow.

"Come on, please. The horses are great. I fed them extra oats in honor of the day."

Not wanting him to see her tears, she ignored him.

"At least veer off to the bunkhouse. It's a helluva lot warmer."

He'd caught up with her, taking her by her shoulders

in an unsuccessful attempt to steer her to his will. But she wanted to see her horses, dammit. She wanted to—

In a move that stole her little remaining breath, Gage swept her off her feet, and into his arms.

"Put me down!" she demanded, bucking against his strength. "You're not in charge of me. Never again will I let anyone take care of—"

"I'm not trying to control you in any way, Jess. Just protect you from yourself—not to mention frostbite."

The snow provided plenty of traction, making the bunkhouse trek no big deal for a man like Gage. Jess continued her struggle to get him to release her, but sensing her attempts were futile, she conserved her energy for delivering a good tongue-lashing.

The bunkhouse was balmy.

But then even if it hadn't have been, the heat of her fury would have had the place toasty soon enough.

Gage dumped her on the bed. "There. You're free. Back in control." His sarcasm-laced tone made her loathe him all the more.

"You don't know what it's like, okay?" Scrambling to a more dignified position, wiping tears from her cheeks, she said, "When you lose someone you love, it's unsettling. Like some malevolent puppet master is jerking your strings. When Dwayne died, I had no control over anything. He'd done the ranch work, paid the bills, hired hands. I've had to learn it all, and I do a damned good job, and you're not just going to waltz in here and take over everything. And now, Christmas is ruined and my daughter's crazy and it won't stop snowing and—" Now that tears had started, they showed no sign of stopping.

"For the record, darlin', yes, I *do* know what losing someone I dearly loved is like. So don't you *dare* sit there, all—"

"Oh, God," she said, crying all the harder. "I—I forgot about your sister."

Gage momentarily vanished, only to return with tissues.

"Thank you, but I—I can get my own Kleenex."

"Of course, you can," Gage said, his tone hard. "My point is that seeing how I'm here, you don't have to." Softening, he added, "If there's anything I've learned over the years, it's that control—over even the small stuff—is an illusion. Lighten up. Let me help with the ranch. That'll give you more time to spend with Lexie. All that girl needs is a whole lot of loving and then—"

"A-are you saying I don't love my daughter?"

"Holy hell in a handbasket, woman. Stop putting words in my mouth. What I'm saying is that you can't do it all. No one can."

"But I *have* to." The gravity of this knowledge slumped her shoulders. "Don't you see? Even if you stayed after the storm, you *will* eventually leave. Then what? I'll be right back where I started. I'll have let my guard down, depended on someone else, and then, bam. I'll be smacked right back to where I started."

Jess took his silence as acknowledgment she was right.

After blowing her nose, she said, "I don't know how my frustration over Lexie led to all of this, but I suppose it had to come out eventually. And I am sorry my daughter ruined Christmas." She shrugged. "There's always next year to get it right."

"For the last time," he said with a low growl, "Lexie hardly ruined Christmas. She doesn't have that power. Christmas is in here…." He settled his hand on her chest, where his warm strength filled her with hope that maybe, someday, Lexie would be herself again and life on the ranch wouldn't be quite so hard.

Tearing up again, she nodded, but knowing his words were true didn't magically erase the way Jess felt. As if her own parental shortcomings had been the sole cause of the mess she now found herself in.

"Ready to head back to the house?" His fingers grazing her chin, Gage raised her eyes to meet his. "If you don't give the all-clear to start opening that pile of presents your folks brought, Ashley's liable to burst."

Sniffling, laughing, Jess knew Gage was yet again right, only this time, his easy smile lessened her pain.

"Thanks," she said.

"For what?"

She shrugged. "Just being here. I know it's only a storm keeping you around, but I'm glad you stayed."

"Me, too…" All at once shocking and thrilling her, he cupped his hand to her cheek. Though her head told her it was a bad idea getting too close, her heart told her to lean in to his touch. To steal the small moment of happiness, and tuck it away to later enjoy.

Chapter Seven

"That's okay," Ashley said into the phone.

Gage assumed she was talking to her paternal grandmother about them having missed sharing Christmas. After both girls had rushed through a half-dozen gifts apiece, Jess had started on her few from her parents. She'd just opened a nice-sized gift card to the local farm-and-ranch supply store when the phone rang.

Once Ashley made her goodbyes, Lexie took a turn.

"Dwayne's folks are good people," Jess said, staring into the fire. "I hate it that they're missing out on Christmas morning."

"Weather happens." Gage nodded toward the window. Snow still fell. "How about New Year's Day, you have a do-over? That way you and the girls get two holidays for the price of one."

Laughing, Jess shook her head. "That's one way to put it."

When Jess took her turn on the phone, Ashley played on the rag rug in front of the fire with her new dinosaur Lego set. Lexie had gotten a new Barbie horse and clothes and enough tiny, plastic shoes to land Gage in the E.R. with back pain should she leave them on his bed.

As for the covered wagon he'd stayed up all night making her, it sat abandoned on one of the kitchen counters. If he left it there, would the girl ever play with it?

Hard to say.

When the weather cleared, he was going to miss Jess and her girls. This old place, with its worn, homey feel. His Dallas condo was only a year old and filled with modern-styled chrome and leather. He spent so much time on the road, the place still smelled of new carpet and paint. His fridge was bare, save for a few skunky beers and fancy condiments Marnie had insisted he have. She'd been sweet like that. Looking after him. Bringing him groceries when she knew he'd be back in town. Lord, how he missed her.

Rubbing the stubble on his jaw, he sighed.

Jess, though still on the phone, caught his gaze. *What's wrong?* she mouthed.

He shook his head. Forced a smile. *Nothing.*

Funny how at the moment, *nothing* could be further from the truth. How had Jess known? Was he that transparent, or was she that in tune with his moods? The very notion was unsettling. No one, save for his mom and Marnie, read him like that. His dad—like him—was generally oblivious.

When he'd called home that morning to wish everyone a merry Christmas, the conversation had been strained. The sadness in his mother's tone had about killed him, which was why he'd cut the call short. No need in torturing her further. Lord knew she had enough reminders of what he'd done each time she looked at one of the dozens of pictures of Marnie.

"Love you, too," Jess said, "we'll see you soon." She hung up, and while the girls played in their own worlds, she said to Gage, "Sorry that took so long. Dwayne's mom—Jeannie—was in the mood to talk."

"It's all right."

"The look on your face a second ago… You didn't look all right."

"Heartburn," he said, fingertips to his chest. "Bacon does it to me every time."

"Then why eat it?"

He shrugged. "It's good." Kind of like the easy give-and-take of hanging out with Jess.

"HE'S LOOKING much better, isn't he?" Jess stood alongside Gage in Honey and Buttercup's stall. Back at the house, the kids were munching popcorn while watching one of their new movies. Christmas had come and gone and while the storm had finally passed, making way for blinding sunlight, the temperature hovered near zero, making the roads as treacherous as ever. Luckily, unlike her parents and Doc, their power hadn't gone out.

Gage nodded, rubbing the sleepy-eyed colt between his ears. "This little guy had me worried. I'm glad he came out of it."

"Me, too." Together, they finished cleaning the stall, then moved on to the next one.

"When's this mare due to foal?" Gage rubbed the sorrel.

"Not 'til mid-January, thank goodness." Jess aimed for the mare's opposite side, giving her nose a pat before filling her water. "What with Honey getting hurt, and Lexie's attitude, I've had all the excitement around here I can take. I wish she were due later, but the stud we used is in high demand, and that was his only opening."

"Lucky guy," Gage said with a chuckle.

Jess rolled her eyes.

It was cold enough in the barn to see their breath, but sharing her daily chores with Gage, Jess hardly noticed the temperature.

"I'm going to miss you," she said once they'd finished. "You're a hard worker."

"I've done no more than you." He perched on a pile of feed bags.

"Sure, but I have to do all of this." She hung the feed bucket on a wall hook beside the bags. "You could be all warm in the bunkhouse. Watching TV or reading a book. You know, just chilling until the roads clear."

"I wasn't raised that way—to *chill* when there's work needing to be done."

Hmm… One more thing to appreciate about him.

"Actually, I've missed being around horses. Up close and personal, like this. I do most of my training on a friend's cattle ranch. I've got a mechanical bull out there, too."

Scratching her head, Jess asked, "Didn't you tell me you're in the off-season?"

"Uh-huh."

"A couple years back, my folks went with Doc and his wife to the Professional Bull Riders World Finals in Vegas. Best as I can recall, it was right before Christmas, because Mom was all upset about getting her shopping done before—"

"We should head back inside," Gage said, hopping up from his makeshift seat. "You've got to be freezing."

"True enough, but seeing how you just used your favorite avoidance technique on me, I'm thinking before we leave this barn, you're going to tell me how it is that you're a pro bull rider, but you didn't just compete in the most important event of the year. And while we're at it, aren't there a few big events in January?"

Jaw hardened, he gazed out at the yard, squinting at the glare. "Let's just say I'm temporarily retired."

"Retired?" She raised her eyebrows.

"That's what I said, isn't it?"

She hefted herself onto the feed sacks where Gage had just been.

"What're you doing?" Thumbs hooked on his Wranglers' back pockets, he said, "Thought we were going inside?"

"We are." She flashed him a sweet smile. "Just as soon as you fill me in on what led you to take early retirement."

Wiping a hand across his face, he shook his head. "It's complicated. I thought we've been over this. Remember how I promised I'm not running from the law?"

"Gage… I don't mean to pry, but you've been so great to the girls and me, maybe I'd like to repay the favor." Rising, she went to him, stopping just short of putting her gloved hands on his back. She wanted to. Lord, how she wanted to. Somehow, it just didn't seem right. Even though she thought of him as a friend, a long-dormant part of her had awoken when they'd kissed, and she knew touching him could only lead to trouble. "You can open up to me, you know? It's not like I'm going to tell anyone. If this is about your sister's death, maybe it'll help whatever's troubling you to—"

"Leave it alone, Jess. Hell, you're like a dog with a bone."

When he went out into the yard, she followed, footsteps crunching the snow. "I don't mean to pry. For what it's worth, I'm worried about you. Guess it's the mom in me."

He veered off toward the bunkhouse. "It's the man in me wishing you'd leave me alone."

She kept pace with him. "I will just as soon as I have some kind of sign you're okay."

"A sign?" He spun to face her so quickly, he nearly slipped and fell.

"See?" she said, catching him by his right arm, almost falling as well from the force of his weight. "You need me."

He snorted. "Like a hole in my head."

"That can be arranged."

"Mooooo-ooooom!" Ashley called, her voice echoing in the cold still. "What's for lunch?"

"We just had breakfast."

"I'm hungry!" the girl insisted.

Sighing, Jess said, "Eat some peanut butter and crackers. I'll be right in to find you something more." To Gage, she mumbled under her breath, "The roads had better clear by the time they go back to school after Christmas break, because I'm not emotionally equipped for added snow days."

"Let me get this straight," Gage said, still holding her arm. "You claim to want to help me, but you can't even handle a little thing like your kids being home from school?"

Jess would've been mad at him for asking such a stupid question, but the twinkle in his eyes told her he was joking. Yanking her arm free, she quipped back, "Fine. If that's the way you feel, I'm officially rescinding my offer."

Expression clouding, he lowered his hand to hold hers. Though they both wore heavy leather work gloves,

Jess would've sworn to feeling the man's radiated heat. "I appreciate the fact that you want to help me, but this…this thing I'm going through has no cure other than maybe time. Hard work."

Gazing up at his rugged, wind-roughened features, Jess bore witness to his eyes tearing. He looked away. Blotted at them with the heel of his free gloved hand.

"We're quite a pair, huh?"

He nodded, and it broke her heart to suspect the reason he didn't answer was because he couldn't speak past the lump in his throat.

She'd vowed earlier to allow him his secrets, so why had she needled him now? He'd be leaving soon enough, meaning she had no right to expect him to open up to her. They'd shared a storm. Christmas. Intimacies that up until now she'd never experienced with a man other than her husband. To her, that was a big deal, but to him—and no doubt, every other living soul—their time together had meant nothing. Why then, couldn't she leave this alone? Leave him alone?

"I, ah—" he cleared his throat "—heard on the radio this morning that it's supposed to warm up tomorrow. Be above freezing for the rest of the week."

"That's great," she said with forced cheer. "I'll bet you're anxious to be home."

After a long, slow exhale, Gage asked, "What are we doing?"

"Excuse me?"

"The small talk. The weather. It's pointless. Fact is, I'm most likely leaving tomorrow, and then what? We never see or talk to each other again?"

"Wh-why would we?" she asked, pulse curiously storming at the very thought of him saying goodbye. He'd been here so short a time, yet she couldn't remember a time when he hadn't been there. Couldn't fathom a time without him there—no matter how inevitable it may be. "Expect to see each other again?"

"Because as crazy as it sounds, I— Oh, hell." Jerking his hand free, he walked away.

"What, Gage?" Not daring to go after him, she cried, "What were you going to say?"

"Your daughter's hungry," he said. "Get her some soup, or mac and cheese."

"What're you going to do?"

"Take a nap."

More likely, when he'd practically slammed the bunkhouse door in her face, Jess figured his true plan was to escape her.

"YOU'RE FUN," ASHLEY SAID, patting her snowman's head.

After a tense lunch of soup and sandwiches, Gage had planned on napping away the rest of the day, but when he'd seen the munchkin outside playing by herself, his heart had gone out to her.

The late afternoon sun shone, but didn't share much warmth. What it did do was turn the world to sparkling crystal. Tree branches too thin to hold snow were ice-drizzled, transforming ordinary scrub oaks into glowing works of art. As kids, he and Marnie used to play in the snow. Build forts and stage epic snowball fights with the neighboring boys down the road.

Ashley said, "This is the best snowman I've ever done. Thanks for getting it so big."

"You're welcome." Standing back to survey their work, he said, "He is pretty cool. Think your mom's got a carrot for his nose?"

"Prob'ly. He needs a hat, scarf and eyeballs, too. And a mouth."

"Tell you what," he said, kneeling to her eye level, "I'll scrounge in the barn for the eyeballs and mouth, and you handle the rest, okay?"

"Meet you back here in five minutes!" Cheeks rosy red, Ashley raced off toward the house. The kid was adorable. Not unlike her mother, but in a much different way.

Trudging through the snow to the barn, Gage thanked his lucky stars that he'd stopped himself from admitting just how much he'd like to keep seeing Jess and her girls. Something about the three of them made life bearable. Not that he was anywhere near forgiving himself, but since he'd been here, there were so many needy souls to tend to that he'd forgotten to dwell on his own issues.

In the storage room, he found a cobwebbed barbecue grill and a dusty bag of charcoal briquettes. Squatting to grab a few, he winced. Now in his thirties, it seemed like his pain tolerance wasn't what it used to be. The cold had returned bodily aches he'd hoped long gone.

His condo had a patio hot tub. Maybe once he got home, he'd spend a few weeks soaking. With no distractions, he'd have plenty of time for getting his body back in shape. His head, however, might prove more difficult.

"I hate you! Why are you so mean?"

When crying followed shouting, Gage hightailed it to the yard. "What's— Oh."

The snowman Ashley had been so proud of had been reduced to a pile of icy crumbles.

Lexie stood nearby, arms crossed, her scowl more fierce than ever. "You're just a stupid kid! Nobody plays in the snow anymore!"

"I do!" Ashley gave her big sister a shove. "I hate you! Why didn't you die instead of Daddy?"

Gage cringed.

When Lexie shoved back, and Ashley started wildly smacking, Gage inserted himself into the center of the battle, ignoring the stings of open-handed slaps landing against him instead of their intended targets.

"That's enough," he said, finally separating them. "Lexie, what's the matter with you? Why would you smash your sister's snowman?"

"It was stupid! And I don't have to talk to you."

"No, you don't," Gage admitted, "but you do owe Ashley an apology. She's worked an hour out here, and was really proud."

Lexie kicked at the snowman's remains. "It's stupid, and so are you!"

Counting to ten in his head, it took everything Gage had in him not to give the smart-mouthed kid a piece of his mind. He got the fact that she was hurting, but why did she have to take out her pain on Ashley? As sour as Lexie was, Ashley was that sweet.

"You're the stupid one!" Ashley hollered right back. "When I tell Mommy about this, she's going to ground you *forever.*"

"What do I care?" Lexie called over her shoulder, flouncing across the yard. "It's not like I can go any-where anyway."

Ashley started in again with her crying.

Gage wasn't sure whether to hug her or chase after Lexie. While he stood there, trying to decide, Jess barreled out the door.

"What's going on out here?" she asked, gravitating toward sobbing Ashley. "I've been paying bills, and heard you two all the way from my office."

"L-Lexie smashed m-my snowman, and then she said she hates me."

"I *do* hate you!" Lexie screamed from an ice- and snow-coated tire swing she'd climbed onto, and was now standing on top of. "I hate all of you! If Daddy was here, he'd— *Aggghh!*" She slipped and fell, and judging by her left arm's angle, she'd snapped it clear in two.

"Oh, my God, Lexie…" Hands covering her gaping mouth, it took Jess a second to react.

In Gage's line of business, busted arms were practically a weekly occurrence with at least someone on the pro circuit. He'd seen guys get their arm in a cast, then be back on a bull the next night. The one thing he hadn't seen, however, was a wailing nine-year-old, her pretty face scrunched in pain.

Whereas moments earlier, he'd been frustrated as hell with the kid, he now scooped her into his arms, carrying her to his truck. To Jess, he shouted, "Grab my wallet and keys from my nightstand, would you? We need to get this kiddo to a doctor."

"But how are you going to drive in this snow?" she asked, cupping Lexie's tearstained cheeks. "Shouldn't I call an ambulance?"

"By the time they make it out here, we could already have Lexie treated. Trust me. There's enough snow over the ice that we should get some traction."

Not looking entirely convinced, Jess kissed her daughter's forehead, then smoothed back her hair.

"I didn't really mean I want you to die," Ashley said to her sister, looking stricken.

Lexie ignored her, upping the volume of her sobs.

"Jess," he said, "the sooner you get my keys, the sooner we get this little one to a doctor."

Eyes wet and huge, she nodded, dashing off to the bunkhouse.

"Ashley," Gage said, "I need you to please grab Lexie's blanket. That pink one she wraps up in while watching movies."

"'Kay."

"How're you doing?" Gage asked Lexie with Ashley running off.

"Bad."

He chuckled, not doubting the kid's pain. He'd suffered three broken arms in his fifteen years of riding. He considered himself lucky for not having had more. "We'll get you fixed up soon."

He wanted to talk more with her about what had led her to kick her sister's snowman, but figured now wasn't the time.

"Here," Jess said, out of breath and holding up his requested items. "Where's Ash?"

While they settled Lexie with a minimum of motion on the truck's cold vinyl seat, Gage explained about having sent her on a mission.

"Ouch!" Lexie railed while Gage fastened her seat belt. "Why won't you let my mom take care of me? Why are you even here?"

Good question, Gage thought, climbing behind the wheel.

"I'm back!" Ashley hopped in the passenger side, tossing Lexie her blanket.

"Ow!" Lexie howled, favoring her arm.

Jess was about to climb in, when she smacked her forehead. "I need my purse. It's got my insurance card. Oh—and I should call Doctor Madison. Let him know we're coming."

Gage started the engine, anxious to get Lexie some heat.

"Th-this is your fault," Lexie said on the heels of

teary hiccups, her statement clearly directed toward him. "If you h-hadn't come, I wouldn't be hurt."

Lips pressed tight, Gage gripped the wheel as hard as he could. This girl was one tough cookie.

"Shut up, Lex," Ashley said. Pulling her carved dino from her coat pocket, she added, "I think Mister Gage is nice."

"Y-you would."

Ashley stuck out her tongue.

Lexie returned the favor.

"I don't think you're really even sick," Ashley taunted. "You're not even bleeding. If you were *really* sick, then your guts would be hanging out all over the place."

"Shut up!" Lexie hollered.

"Faker!" Ashley taunted.

"Ugly!"

"Both of you, knock it off." Gage shot them his meanest look. "I swear, you two sound like a couple of rabid coon dogs, intent on tearing each other apart."

"Sorry," Ashley said, chin hugging her chest.

Lexie closed her eyes, feigning sleep.

Jess came running up to the truck, creaking open the passenger-side door.

Gage had a better ride back in his Dallas garage, but it was the vehicle he used for touring, and being back in it reminded him of Marnie and how she used to tag along with him on her breaks from the University of Texas. This old clunker had seen better days, but was a workhorse.

"Know the way to town?" Jess asked.

"Yep." He put the truck in Reverse and eased it back. At first, the tires spun, but he rocked it a couple times until the wheels rolled above the snow.

The sun had nearly set, streaking the sky orange and purple. Under different circumstances, the beauty of it would've made for pleasant conversation. Now, however, it just reminded him how little daylight there was to guide him through fifteen inches of snow-topped ice.

The tires hit a slick patch, and before he'd even reached the road, the vehicle fishtailed before making a terrifying sideways slide.

Chapter Eight

While Lexie and Ashley screamed, Jess used one hand to brace herself against the dash, and held her other in front of the girls. Gage did the same, only with one hand keeping a white-knuckled grip on the wheel.

In an instant, he'd regained control. "Everyone all right?"

"Yeah," Ashley said, "but that was scary. Let's not do it again."

"Deal." Gage eased the truck onto the road.

"D-Daddy wouldn't have crashed us," Lexie mumbled.

Jess sighed.

Gage stopped the truck, then angled to face Lexie. "Look, Tater Tot, I get the fact that you don't like me. I also get it that you wish you could trade me in for your dad. But you need to get it through your thick skull that I'm not trying to take his place. All I want to do is help your mom with the ranch and get you to town. Now, will you lay off and let me drive?"

A minute later, Gage regretted his harsh words, but dammit, all he was trying to do was help, and all she kept giving him was grief. Was he really such a wretched guy?

How about asking your sister?

Great. Putting the crowning touch on an already crappy day, his conscience had to go butting in, reminding him just what a screwup he really was. Oh, he might be doing a good deed in hauling Little Miss Mouth to the doctor, but that didn't erase what was already done—the fact that he'd essentially handed over his sister to the worst kind of tragedy of all.

"How is she?" Gage asked once Jess left the doctor's exam room, while Lexie was still inside. He and Ashley had been in the dimly lit waiting room, their only company being the fish colony residing in an impressive, wall-size saltwater aquarium. The underwater theme continued with blue walls and blue upholstered chairs and plenty of cartoon-style fish pictures.

Ashley had long since fallen asleep in an awkward, sideways position that if she weren't a kid would have her mighty sore when she woke.

"She'll be all right," Jess said, exhaustion deadening her tone. "It's a simple break. The doctor said her cast should be off in about ten weeks."

"That's good," he said. "Did he give her something for pain?"

Jess nodded. "He's just now finishing the cast. I had to use the restroom, and saw you sitting out here, and…" Fumbling her hands at her waist, she seemed to struggle for her next words. "I, well, thank you for driving us. I've never been much good in the snow. The year Dwayne… Well, we haven't had much in the way of bad weather in a while."

"Glad I could help," Gage said. In a way, her gratitude warmed him, but in another, it hurt. Plainly, she needed him.

What would've happened had he not been there to drive Lexie? As much as his ego wanted to deny it, probably nothing, other than the girl would've been in pain a little longer. Either an ambulance would've made its way out to the ranch, or Jess would've gotten hold of a neighbor with four-wheel drive.

Truth was, it was Gage needing Jess and her girls.

"Well…" She was at it again with her hand flopping. "Guess I should head back to Lexie."

"Jess?" he asked.

"Yes?" The bluish glow of the aquarium's light lent her an ethereal glow. Never had she looked more beautiful. Never had he needed her more. Just a hug. A kind word. Something to tell him everything was going to be okay.

It was on the tip of his tongue to just come out and ask her if he could stay with her and the girls on the ranch, but in the end, the words wouldn't come. He'd never considered himself an overly prideful man, but something about groveling at the woman's feet, begging her to lend him even a few more days' sanity, struck an errant chord. He was a grown man, for Christ's sake. He needed to pull himself up by his bootstraps and get the hell on with his life.

"Gage?" she prompted. "Did you want to ask me something?"

"Nah," he said, shoving his hands in his pockets before sharply looking away. "I'm good."

Only as she cast him a faint smile, he realized he was anything but good. Seeing Lexie hurt had served as a reminder to just how fragile life could be.

"I'm glad," she said softly. "One of us needs to be alert. God knows it isn't me."

"LEXIE ASLEEP?" Gage asked thirty minutes after they'd gotten home. It was pushing ten, yet even after the long drive, he was hard at work, insuring the house was warmed by a healthy fire.

Jess nodded. "Ashley, too."

Seated on the stone hearth, Gage stared into dancing flames. "Man, it's been a long, weird day."

"Long, yes," she said, sitting beside him, soaking in the heat, "but how was it weird?"

He half laughed. "That's right, you missed Lexie's act of terrorism."

"Her *what?*"

"Ashley and I had just built a snowman, and were putting on the finishing touches, when Lexie came along and smashed it to oblivion."

Jess groaned. "She didn't?"

"Oh, yes. She did. A screaming slap-fest then ensued, followed by Ashley telling her sister she wished she'd died instead of their dad."

Hand clamped to her forehead, Jess closed her eyes. "Could my life get worse?"

"It technically could," he said, nudging her knee, "but I wouldn't recommend it."

"Ha-ha." She nudged him back. "Seriously, Gage, sometimes I feel like I'm stuck in a bad dream. Even after Lexie was hurt, she didn't drop her wall. I don't know what to do to get through to her."

"Give it time," he said, as he went back to staring into the fire.

"Yeah." She yawned.

"Am I that exciting?"

"Sorry," she said with a faint grin. "You were right about it being a long day. I'm exhausted. But my brain's going a mile a minute. I doubt I'll be able to sleep."

"Wanna watch a movie?" He used the poker to shift the coals, then added another log to the fire.

"No."

"Want me to make you something to eat?"

Shaking her head, she said, "Thanks, but I'm really not hungry."

"In that case…" Hand on her knee, he gave it a light squeeze. "Our only options are mopping the floors or playing dominos. Your choice."

Taking his hand in hers, she turned it over, tracing his scarred palm. "Why do you ride bulls when it obviously hurts so bad?"

"Why do you keep trying to break through to Lexie?"

"Because I love her?"

"Ding, ding, ding," he teased, mimicking a county fair barker. "Give that lady a prize."

"But Lexie's my daughter. I'd give my life for her. Are you saying you feel that way about riding a stupid bull?"

"When you put it that way…" He laced their fingers together. "I know it sounds crazy, but something about dancing with the devil… It's a powerful thing. My mom hates it. Won't even watch me ride, but I can't stop."

"But you have. Or else you wouldn't be here." She didn't mean to bring up the topic again, but somehow they'd wound around to it. Would he get angry? Ditch her again for the privacy of the bunkhouse?

His jaw hardened.

Here it came, he was getting ready to blow.

Jess steeled herself.

"As hard as it is to admit…" He took a deep breath. Slowly exhaled. "You're right."

"Right?" She coughed. Jiggled her ear. "Surely I didn't hear you correctly?"

"Hey…" he complained, stroking her palm, filling her with thoughts she didn't want, but couldn't stop. Thoughts of him moving his touch higher. Holding her, kissing her, making her forget. Making her whole and happy and alive. "I'm trying to be serious here."

"Sorry," she said with a slight shake of her head, wishing she were anywhere but here. Knowing it would take an act of God to move her from this very spot. "By all means, continue."

"I would, only I'm not sure what I'm trying to say."

"Maybe that you're ready to retire? At least from riding?" His expression was a blank slate. Dark, but not angry or sad. Just empty. Spent, like he'd been through more than he could bear. Had he suffered a nasty fall? Been gored, and only just now recovered? No. Judging by how hard he worked and how fit he seemed, that theory didn't make sense.

"Yeah," he said with a firm nod. "That must be it. I've had enough, and am ready to try something new."

"Like what?"

"Heck, how should I know?" Releasing her hand, he stood and paced.

"Have you had any college? Work experience in anything but rodeo or ranching?"

"Nope."

"Well…" Her breath coming in short hitches, she said not what she should have, but what she wanted to. "I suppose you could always stay on here. I could take a gamble on you working out." On maybe sticking around just long enough to help her get back on her financial feet. His staying would be purely for the ranch. The horses. Nothing at all to do with making her pulse race. Or carving the perfect dinosaur or covered wagon or carrying her so her feet didn't get cold or driving an hour one way through drifting snow to get her little girl to a doctor. "And in the spirit of you being honest with me, Gage…I don't think you staying would be all that much of a gamble. In fact, after tonight, you've shown me that maybe I do need help. I can't do it all—or even come close. If I'd had to drive Lexie tonight, I don't know what would've happened. We'd have probably ended up in a ditch and frozen to death, but—"

"Shh." Hands on her shoulders, he drew her up, until his lips covered hers and her knees threatened to buckle. "What am I doing?"

"Don't stop," she whispered, quivering from the force of her feelings—whatever they may be. It'd been so long since she'd been held. She wasn't talking about being hugged by her mom or dad or the girls, but by a man. Someone strong and tall and who made her feel not like someone capable of caring for a ranch all on her own. But like a woman.

"I have to," he said, kissing her once more before gently pushing her away. "Just like I have to go first thing in the morning. I'm no good for you, Jess. I'm bad news who should just—"

Damn him. If he wouldn't kiss her, she'd just kiss him. On tiptoes, she took what she wanted. At least until Gage again pushed her away.

"What's wrong with me?" she asked, determined not to give in to the knot walling her throat. "Why don't you want me?"

"Aw, Jess…" Rubbing his hand over his jaw, he said, "If only I didn't want you. This—whatever it is—would be so much easier. You have to understand that I'm no good for you. You deserve better. A guy like your Dwayne. A family man who doesn't spend ninety percent of his life on the road, and the other ten busted up in some hospital bed. Hell, half the time I wake up not even sure what town I'm in."

"You said yourself you're tired of that life, Gage."

"True. But that doesn't mean I have a clue what kind of life I do want."

"Liar."

"What?"

"You heard me. Know what I think?"

"No," he said with a sarcastic chuckle, "but I'm sure you're about to tell me."

"What I think," she said with a defeated, teary smile, "is that with every busted bone in your body, you want to stay here with me and the girls, but you're scared."

"Damn straight I'm scared. You don't know where I've been. What I've done."

"And a few minutes ago, Gage, I didn't care. But now…" She shook her head, spinning away from him so he wouldn't see her tears. Not to mention her secret shame at having thrown herself at him. "I think you were right. You should definitely go."

Chapter Nine

Gage woke to light streaming through the bunkhouse's paned windows. For the first time in days, the sun brought warmth, and the whole world sounded as if it were dripping.

The lead in his stomach told him he should already be on the road. But the lead in his legs wouldn't let him move.

Could he have botched things worse with Jess?

Why should he care? He'd come here to hide out. Lick his wounds. Bury himself in hard work and fresh air. Not some woman's soft hold. Surely not in the adorable giggles of one little girl and the challenging glower of another.

He showered and brushed his teeth.

Shoved all of his crap in a duffel.

Not knowing whether it'd be easier for Jess if he stripped his bed or made it, he compromised with stripping the sheets and folding the quilt.

Taking one last look around the place for old time's sake, he slapped his hat on his head, then walked out the door. He stashed his bag in the truck bed before trudging through the slop in the yard, and on up to the barn. Jess would have her hands full, catering to Lexie's needs. He'd overslept, and was getting a late start on chores, but better late than never.

The once beautiful snow looked pockmarked and dirty.

All of the ice had melted from the trees.

It was only seven-thirty, but judging by the rate of thaw, the temperature had to already be in the forties.

In the barn, Honey greeted him with a soft neigh.

"How are you doing, bud?" Gage rubbed the colt between his ears. "Ready for breakfast?"

"He's already been fed," Jess said, coming out of Smoky Joe's stall, loaded pitchfork in hand. "As has everyone else."

Removing his hat, Gage asked, "Why didn't you wake me? I overslept, but would've been happy to handle the chores while you tended to Lexie."

"She's still sleeping." After dumping her load in a wheelbarrow, she then wheeled it out the side door, aiming for the still snow-covered manure pile.

He followed, tossed his hat on a pile of feed sacks, then bumped her out of the way so that he could take over the load. "It's supposed to get in the low fifties today, Jess, so what's up with your frosty tone?"

"I have no tone, and I can manage," she said, small, work-roughened hands over his. They were red and calloused and chapped. Not the hands of the rodeo queens with whom he usually hung out. He'd arrived on her ranch not only to escape his own problems, but also to help out someone with troubles of her own. So what was he doing leaving?

"Where are your gloves?" he asked.

"I was preoccupied with getting Lexie her pain medicine and forgot them down at the house." Wrestling him for control of the wheelbarrow's handles, she said, "Hadn't you better get on the road?"

"I will. In my own good time. Now, scoot."

"No," she said, bearing down all the more until they were both hunched over, shoulder to shoulder, fighting over the rights to wheel the big old pile of dung.

"Yes," he said, equally determined to get his way.

"No."

"I'll do it," he demanded.

"No, me," she declared right back.

After both barely managed to squeeze side-by-side through the door, the race was on, only with added space to maneuver, Gage was pretty sure he had the battle won.

At least until Jess fought dirty by tripping him.

"What the—" Down he went, but seeing how he'd taken hold of her on the way down, she landed atop him.

For the longest time, she just lay there, silently fuming, breathing hard. But then she met his gaze, and he hers, and something about the lunacy of their situation brought on a grin.

"What's so funny?" she snapped.

"Hell, woman, you feel so good riding me, how can I help but smile?"

With a frustrated growl, she tried pushing herself off him, but he'd clamped his arms around her and wasn't about to let go. It didn't matter that snow had soaked clear through the seat of his jeans. Didn't matter that he no doubt looked a fool. All that did matter was that if he had even so much as an ounce of gentleman left in him, no matter what this redheaded hellion said, he wasn't about to let the sight of her poor, work-roughened hands keep him up nights.

"Let me go," she insisted.

"Nope."

"Why not?" she asked, struggling all the harder.

"Because I'm getting the feeling that you, like your stubborn-as-a-crotchety-old-mule daughter, need just as much taming."

"Taming?" She coughed as if choking on her own spit. "That's the craziest thing I've ever heard. Not to mention, rude."

"Yeah, well—" he shifted to make them both more comfortable, not to mention ease the growing pressure beneath his fly "—haven't you heard the expression 'nice guys finish last'?"

Renewing her struggles, she said, "You're obviously not the nice guy I thought you were."

"Oh," he said with a laugh, "but that's where you're wrong. Because I *am* such a good guy, whether you want me here or not, I'm staying."

"Y-you what?" She froze.

"You heard me. While I fully acknowledge you are capable of doing everything around here, in all good conscience, I can't let you. You've got a sick munchkin to look after and another one craving attention. Go to them, Jess." Pulling off his glove, softening his hold, he smoothed back flyaways that'd escaped her already messy ponytail. "Let me shoulder just a fraction of all you have to do, and I'll bet Lexie snaps right out of her funk."

"I can't," Jess said, her defeated posture belying her strong words.

"Why not?"

She took her sweet time finding an answer. "Like I said before, what if you do stay, and I do end up giving you more and more of my load? What happens when you get bored with all of us, and defeat whatever demons you're chasing and start itching to get back out on the road?"

"Not going to happen," he assured her, even though a small part of him wrestled with the notion of her possibly being right.

"Easy enough to say, but can you promise?"

No. Moreover, he'd never be able to give her what she'd craved the previous night. She'd practically begged him to kiss her, hold her, never let her go. But he was no good for her. Oh, sure, he could shoulder more than his fair share of the work, but when it came to giving Jess what he suspected she really needed—a man to hold her through the night—it wasn't in his power.

"Gage?" Her stare said it all—that she wanted with every fiber of her being to trust him not to hurt her, but she was scared. Well, dammit, he was scared, too, but not because he feared he'd hurt her. He knew if he didn't maintain his distance, causing her pain was a certainty.

"Tell you what," he said, struggling to get them both back on their feet. "*If* I ever decide to go back to rodeoing, I promise to provide you with a replacement. Fair enough?"

"What if I can't afford to pay him?"

"I'll make up the difference. Put it in writing if you want."

"Why, Gage? Why would you do that?"

Because I'm afraid I've fallen for you? The truth landed a good, hard kick to his stomach. "Why? Because it's the right thing to do. Because I wasn't raised to turn away a woman or children in need." *Most importantly, because selfishly, being here, for the first time in months, I can wrap my hands around someone else's problems for a change and, if only for a small part of the day, put aside mine.*

Gazing up at the sky, she let loose a groan.

"What's that mean?"

"That you confuse me," she said, looking him in the eyes. "Part of me wants you to stay, but not because you feel some sense of duty or obligation. I…" She lowered her gaze and dragged in a breath. "I want you to stay, Gage, because you *want* to. Because you can't imagine being anywhere but here. But I hardly know you so the very idea of you feeling that way is ridiculous, and—"

"Jess." He took her hands in his. "The last time you rambled on like this, I kissed you quiet, but I promised myself I wasn't going to do that kind of thing anymore, so all I can do is promise you—with everything in me— that if you do take a gamble on me… You'll win. Shoot, we'll both win."

"I—I think so, too," she said. "So now there's only one problem."

"What's that?"

She cleared her throat. "It's not so much an it, but a *who*."

Now Gage was the one groaning. "Let me guess… Lexie?"

NEW YEAR'S EVE, Jess sat on the living-room sofa, sandwiched by two snoozing girls. It was only ten, but she figured what with Gage having vanished thirty minutes earlier to check the horses, she might as well hit the sack, too.

Above the soft crackle of the fire and the New Year's Times Square special on TV, Jess heard the back door creak open, then close. Shortly thereafter, Gage appeared, his hair loveably mussed, and that slow grin of his making her crazy with wanting.

"Took you long enough," she complained.

"That a problem?"

"Yes," she said, not meaning to be cranky, but secretly disappointed in having been abandoned on New Year's Eve. "You already checked them once."

Removing his work jacket and gloves, he warmed himself by the fire. "Truth be told, I wasn't in the barn, but the bunkhouse."

Oh—that made her feel much better.

"Aren't you going to ask what I was doing?"

"None of my business," she said, trying not to be sullen. After all, it wasn't as if he was her date. Or anything, for that matter, other than her employee and friend.

"Actually," he teased, "it sort of is your business, seeing how what I was doing was setting up the gift I wanted to give you on Christmas, but it never quite worked out."

"A gift? For me?" As if she hadn't already felt ridiculous about having copped an attitude with him, now Jess felt about as low as her busted porch rail hugging the ground.

"Why so surprised? You deserve a present, don't you?"

"Not really."

Waving off her comment, he said, "Right now, go get your coat on, then head out to the bunkhouse. I'll stay with the girls."

"But—"

He crossed the room, taking her by her hands to urge her off the sofa. "Go."

"All right," she said, "but this is a little weird."

"Weird?" He laughed. "For that, I should take back my gift. Obviously, you're not worthy."

No, she wasn't. But that was neither here nor there.

"Go," he repeated with a gentle squeeze of her hands. "And don't come back for at least an hour."

Now she was really confused. But in the spirit of his contagious smile, she went along with the fun.

The air outside was crisp, making it tough going through the yard's frozen ruts. By the time she'd reached the bunkhouse, her teeth were chattering.

She pushed open the door and gasped.

The place glowed with a fire dancing in the wood-stove.

In the bathroom, an odd assortment of household candles made the steam rising from the bubble-filled tub extra special. A note taped to the medicine cabinet read:

> *Merry late Christmas, Jess! You told me you don't have time to pamper yourself, well, now that I'm here to stay, you officially do. Have fun!*

Tears welled in Jess's eyes as she worried her lower lip. No one had ever done anything so thoughtful for her. No one. Was Gage a ranch hand or an angel?

Still shivering from the outside's cold, she made quick work of stripping her clothes.

Dipping one foot under the water, she found the temperature just right, and climbed the rest of the way in. Lying back, closing her eyes, her skin tingled and hummed with pleasure. It'd been years since she'd partaken in such an indulgence.

One of the candles must've been vanilla, as the rich scent filled the room.

Eyes open, she lifted her right foot from the water, happily wriggling her toes. Naked toes that would look much better with shiny red polish. That was another indulgence she'd given up. But no more. Thanks to Gage, she now had time to not only be a mom, but also a woman.

"WHAT ARE YOU DOING HERE?" Lexie had woken, and she didn't look at all pleased to find Gage had replaced her mother. He'd long since carried Ashley up to her room. "Where's my mom?"

"She's busy," he said. "Ready for bed?"

"It's New Year's Eve. I get to stay up as late as I want."

"Then how come you've been sleeping since ten, and it's now pushing twelve?"

Her only answer was to stick out her tongue.

"Lexie Margaret—upstairs. Now." Jess entered the living room, unwrapping her scarf from around her neck.

"But it's New Year's," the girl sassed. "I always get to stay up."

"Not with this kind of attitude." Pointing toward the stairs, she said, "Move it."

"I hate you," Lexie grumbled.

"I love you," Jess hollered. "Whew," she said to Gage once her daughter was out of earshot. "Now that that's settled, has anyone ever told you you're a saint?"

"Not that I can recall." He reclaimed his seat on the sofa. "But I'll be proud to wear the title. Have fun?"

Collapsing next to him, she grinned. "I can't ever remember feeling more relaxed. How did you know that was exactly what I needed? I mean, seriously, how could such a simple thing as sitting in hot water dissolve so much angst?"

Shrugging, he said, "All I know is that when my muscles are screaming, I've always enjoyed a good soak."

"Thank you," she said, shocking him with a kiss to his cheek. "That was an incredibly thoughtful gift. One I'll remember for many years to come."

"Good. That was what I'd hoped."

"Hey, look." She pointed to the TV, where the giant crystal ball had started to drop. "Six," she said, counting along.

"Five…" Gage took a turn.

"Four…" She couldn't help but gravitate closer to him.

"Three…" He moved an infinitesimal bit closer to her.

"Two…" Their lips were now close enough that she felt his heat.

"One…" He took her hands, caressing her palms with his thumbs.

"Happy New Year," she whispered.

"Happy New Year," he whispered back.

The tension between them was a sizzling, palpable thing. Gage ached to kiss the woman, but stayed true to his vow to remain friends. *Just* friends. No matter how much that vow was killing him inside—or, more specifically, beneath his fly.

"THAT WAS A FINE MEAL," Clive Cummings said to his wife, Jeannie, patting her behind as she refilled everyone's iced tea. Though it was New Year's Day, everyone was considering it their *do-over* Christmas.

"Amen," said Georgia. "Absolutely delicious."

"Best ham I've had in years," Jess's dad said.

Jess, Gage, Doc and Martha all seconded that opinion.

"Thank you." Jeannie bustled around the cramped, lilac-themed dining room. When the leaf was in the table, there wasn't much space for maneuvering. When Jess and Dwayne had first started dating, his mom sat them at a kid table to conserve space. "I just hate it that we're a week late celebrating the biggest day of the year."

"It's okay, Gramma," Ashley said, bringing a forkful of mashed potatoes to her lips. "It still tastes good even though it's old."

Everyone at the table laughed.

Everyone, that is, save for Lexie.

"Better late than never is what I always say." Jess's dad helped himself to three more rolls.

Jeannie truly had outdone herself.

The two-story, antique-filled farmhouse had never looked better. All decked out for Christmas, with two live trees. One glittered with family-made ornaments and colorful lights. The other was elegant with white lights and ornaments of silver and gold. The dinner of ham and cheesy hash browns and all the trimmings had been delicious, and the company was welcome after having spent so long cooped up in the house.

The one oddity about the day—well, aside from Lexie's perma-scowl—was Gage. And the fact that Jess secretly craved him more than Jeannie's legendary pecan pie.

Gage looked amazing in a white shirt and tie, and clean jeans. He'd spent a lot of time outdoors, and his ruddy complexion was sun-kissed. Speaking of kisses, she couldn't get theirs out of her mind. No matter how much she needed to keep hold of her emotions, having him take control of her like that had been heady. Shameful. But there it was.

Good grief. Hands to her flaming cheeks, she prayed no one at the table would notice.

"Jess, dear," asked Jeannie, "you all right? You look flushed."

"I'm, um, fine," she lied. "Just waiting for all I've eaten to settle so I can start on seconds."

"Gage—" Clive held a candied pineapple ring in one hand and an asparagus stalk in the other "—when Doc and I were out to the ranch the other day looking in on Honey, I've gotta say the place looked great. My boy would be proud."

"Thank you, sir."

Doc asked, "And have you ever seen that woodpile healthier?"

"Have you been warm enough in the bunkhouse?" Georgia wanted to know.

"Yes, ma'am. It's plenty warm."

"Good." Georgia buttered a corn bread muffin. "Martha, Jeannie and I worked hard getting that depressing little place fixed up. I'd hate to think after all of that effort, you weren't comfortable."

"Really, I'm good."

While conversation went on around her, Jess leaned in toward Lexie, whispering in her ear, "Sweetie, you haven't eaten much. Arm hurting?"

She nodded.

"You can have pain medicine in an hour. Want to lie down until then?"

"No. I just wanna go home."

"But we haven't even finished supper. And Grandma Jeannie made all of her special pies. Even blueberry, just for you."

"I don't like it anymore." With her good hand, she swirled her mashed potatoes with her hash browns.

"Stop playing with your food," Jess said. "It's not polite."

"Like it's polite for everyone Daddy loved to be all gushy over stupid Gage?"

"What was that?" Jeannie asked Lexie. "I didn't hear you, hon."

To Jess's everlasting horror, her daughter was only too happy to repeat every word, finishing with, "Daddy would hate all of you for being nice to *him*." She pointed at Gage.

"That's enough," Clive said. "Young miss, any more hateful talk like that, and I'll wash your mouth out with soap."

"She didn't mean it," Jeannie said with an indulgent smile.

"Yes, I did," Lexie said, shoving her chair back so hard that it tipped. "I hate him!"

Jess started to get up, but her mother—seated to her right—gently urged her down. "Let her go. She'll be fine."

"I'm not so sure," Jess said.

"Maybe it'd be best if I went on home," Gage said.

"You mean back to the ranch?" Doc asked.

"No. I mean, home. Dallas. The last thing I wanted to do here was break a little girl's heart, and that's obviously what's happening with Lex."

"Nonsense," Clive said. "We've all had to deal with my son's passing. There's not a day goes by I don't think of him, but that doesn't give me the right to go spouting off to anyone passing by. Now, Gage, I realize we hardly know each other, but would you mind if I shared a piece of advice?"

"No, sir," Gage said with a respectful bow of his head. "I'd welcome anything you care to share."

"All right then—you ask me, stay put. No offense, Jess, but the ranch looks good, which does my heart good. Darlin',," he said, blowing Jess a kiss, "bless your soul, I know you've put everything you have into making a go of the place, but like me and everyone else at this table have been saying for months, you just can't do it all on your own."

With a strangled laugh, Jess said, "Um, thanks, Clive. I'm glad you think so highly of me."

"Oh, now, don't go getting your panties in a wad." He snatched another pineapple ring from the ham. "Sweetheart, you know I love you, but you need help. There's no shame in that. My boy never meant for you to be riding fences and mucking stalls. He intended you to be raising his babies, and from the sound of that sassy youngun' you might want to spend less time with your horses and a whole lot more time with her."

"Beats anything I've ever seen." On horseback a couple of days later, surveying the newest load of junk that'd been dumped into the valley where Honey had been hurt, Gage took off his hat, using it to wipe sweat from his brow. Leave it to Oklahoma to have a blizzard one week, then be in the seventies the next. "You ever call the law?"

"Sure," Jess said, riding Smoky Joe, "but they tell me since it's privately owned land, unless I find proof of who's doing this, their hands are tied."

In addition to all of the barbed wire that'd been left the last time, there was now a sofa with springs sticking out where there used to be cushions, an old washing machine, about fifteen tires and a bunch of assorted household garbage spewing from torn black trash bags. Not only did the mess look bad, but it also stank like spoiled milk and rotten meat.

"Tell you what," Gage said, "seeing how it's about

time for the girls' school bus, you ride on back to the house. I'm going to sort through some of those bags. See if I can find junk mail or something else with a name on it."

"There's not that much to go through. How about letting me help?"

Already off his horse, tying the buckskin's reins to a fence post, Gage said, "I'd really rather you head on back. This is man's work."

Rolling her eyes, Jess dismounted, as well. "Man's work? Who do you think did this kind of thing before you got here?"

"Yes," he said, tying her horse's reins, "but now I'm here, and I'd prefer you keep your hands clean."

"That's mighty gallant of you, sir, but seeing how this is my land, I'm not above getting good and dirty."

"Hmm… Good to know." He winked.

She smacked him. "Get your mind out of the gutter, cowboy."

"You said it."

"Yeah, but you thought it."

Plenty of good-natured banter carried them through the chore, but unfortunately, to no avail. Thirty minutes later, and they'd been through all of the bags.

"What now, boss?" Sitting back on his haunches, Gage looked up at Jess. Her hair shone fiery in the sun. Lord, but she was a fine-looking woman. Tall and slender, but no longer skinny. He'd always preferred a woman who had a little meat on her bones.

"Guess we'd better return to the house. We'll come back here in a few days. See if there's anything new."

"Sounds good."

They'd ridden about halfway home when Gage summoned the nerve to ask, "About Sunday dinner…"

"What about it?"

"You're kidding, right?" He shot her a sideways glance. "Am I the only one who picked up on the vibe?"

"You mean the one where everyone sang your praises? And acted like the past year I've done nothing but sit on my behind gobbling bonbons?"

"So then you know what I'm talking about? It was weird. Like they all wanted me here—badly."

"They worry. About the girls. Me. The horses. Lord knows, my woodpile." Her sideways grin crinkled the corners of her eyes. With his fingertips, he wanted to trace those crinkles. Kiss them. What she didn't realize was that he worried, too. Only about so much more. Not just about Jess and the girls' general well-being, but whether or not he'd be around in the coming months to watch them grow. To hear Ashley spout her next dino fact. To see Jess willingly relinquish some of her duties to take time for herself. To experience the thrill of Lexie actually talking to him or smiling instead of casting killer death rays.

"Sure," he said, "I get it. Worry's a, ah, universal thing." Only trouble was, worry and a dime wouldn't buy you coffee. How many months after the fact had he worried about what had become of Marnie? About what had made him so blind as to what had been going on?

They were almost to the house when the school bus, followed by a low-hanging dust cloud, barreled down the dirt road. How fast things changed. A week and a half earlier, the road had been semifrozen muck.

"Did their comments on Sunday really hurt you?" he asked.

"A little." Leading her horse up the last rise to the barn, she said, "But then I got to thinking…"

"'Bout what?"

"How I kind of want you to stay, too." She glanced sideways at him and her shy smile was so pretty, so brimming with an indefinable something—maybe hope?—that it stole his breath.

With every fiber of his being, Gage wanted to reach out to her. To take her hand, ease his fingers between hers. Drink in her warmth. Call her his own. But that wasn't going to happen any more than Lexie would run off the bus and hold out her arms for a hug.

Chapter Ten

"How was school?" Jess and the girls were getting supper ready, while Gage got the horses settled for the night. "You all dashed out to play with Honey so fast when you got off the bus, we didn't have a chance to talk."

"It was a fun day," Ashley said, adding chopped mushrooms to four salads. "We learned about ponds. I told Mrs. Barnes that we have three, and she said once springtime gets here, she wants me to bring some water so we can look at it under a microscope."

"That sounds neat," Jess said, washing leaf lettuce. "Lexie, hon? How about you?"

"My arm hurt."

"I'm sorry." Patting the lettuce dry, Jess asked, "Aside from your arm hurting, did you learn anything interesting?"

"No."

Breaking the lettuce and putting it in bowls, Jess asked, "Did you have something good for lunch?"

"No."

"Did you at least have fun at recess with your friends?"

Lexie pulled out a kitchen chair and sat down hard. "I don't have any friends."

Lips pressed tight, praying for heavenly guidance, seeing how she was fresh out of ideas on how to coax her daughter from her self-imposed shell, Jess went to the girl. Hugging her from behind and kissing the top of her head, she said, "For what it's worth, sweetheart, I love you. I want to be your friend."

Lexie stiffened. "Yeah, but you want to be Gage's friend more. Everyone in our whole, stupid family does."

"You're the stupid one!" Ashley railed, pitching a mushroom at her sister. "I'm so tired of you! Why can't you just leave?"

"Ashley!" Jess scolded.

"I hate you all!" Lexie screamed. "Either Gage leaves or I'm running away!"

Tears burned Jess's eyes, but she refused to let them fall. Too often as of late, she'd given in to tears, but Lexie's attitude had gotten to the point where she no longer had the luxury of giving in to her own pain. As for her hidden cravings to be closer to Gage, they had to stop.

This afternoon, riding alongside him, his rangy body silhouetted by the vast Oklahoma sky, she'd imagined herself on his horse, seated behind him, clutching his broad chest, resting her cheek between his shoulder blades, losing herself in his strength, allowing him to make everything okay. But in reality, there was no such thing.

Over and over, life had taught her that "okay" didn't exist. "Okay" was the unobtainable pot of gold at the end of the rainbow that mysteriously drifted away whenever one seemed close.

Jess wanted desperately to explore a relationship with Gage that extended beyond friendship, take a journey to a place she never thought she'd visit again.

Because of her daughter's misgivings, that could never happen. Must never happen.

Lexie had already lost so much. She couldn't lose her mother, too. And that's how she'd view Jess getting close to Gage.

"Lexie," Jess said from between gritted teeth, "sweetie, I know you're hurting, that's why I try so hard to be patient when it comes to your temper, but please, try to understand that Gage has been a godsend to me. I need his help."

"You did just fine before *he* got here."

Had she? For the first time in years, the calluses on her hands had begun to soften. Their dinners were more than just instant potatoes, microwaved meat and canned green beans. The kitchen floor was being mopped again and the living room dusted. The laundry pile had fallen to a manageable level and the generally meager wood-pile was as healthy as the horses that were the ranch's lifeblood. All of that, no matter how much it hurt Jess to admit, was due to Gage.

"Think back, Lex. Remember when you and Ashley had to do most of the house chores, because I was always in the barn?"

"But I didn't mind," Lexie said. "At least then, I didn't have to share you."

"What makes you think you have to share me now?" Jess asked. When Lexie said nothing, she coaxed, "Come on, seriously, tell me right this minute a time when you've wanted to be with me, and I wasn't around."

"When I got off the bus today, you weren't out at the road, but in the barn. *With Gage.*"

"Not that it's any of your business, but we were brushing down the horses."

"I think you were *kissing* him."

Jess swallowed her anger. "Go to your room," she said, keeping her hands to her sides so the girl couldn't see how they trembled. "Go to your room, and stay there until you feel like being civil."

When Lexie stormed off, Ashley hopped down from her kitchen stool, wrapping her arms around Jess's waist. "I love you, Mommy."

"Love you, too, hon."

"Mmm…" Gage strolled through the back door, patting his stomach. "What's that delicious smell? I'm starving."

"It's good someone's hungry," Jess said as physical, but mostly mental, exhaustion pressed on her shoulders. "Because at the moment, I don't think I could eat a thing."

"You don't have to do this, you know." The next day, she stood on a step stool, hanging the blue floral living-room curtains she'd just washed, dried and ironed. They'd been so dusty, the colors had actually dulled. Gage was acting as her third hand, handing panels to her whenever she was ready.

"I do know. But it seemed like you needed help."

She gazed down to find his sinfully handsome face dangerously close to her derriere. Cheeks flaming, she tried ignoring his proximity. Tried. Then her imagination noted how easy it would be to hop off the stool and into his arms. Maybe even have him lift her high enough to wrap her arms around his neck and her legs around his waist. Then they'd kiss. Slow at first, but building in intensity until she was dizzy with need. And then—

"You all right?" he asked, holding up the next section of curtain.

"Um, sure," she said, licking her tingling lips. "I'm great." Taking the frilly fabric, she was only too happy to face the wall's cool anonymity.

"You look all red and splotchy."

"Gee, thanks. You're great for my ego."

She glanced over her shoulder to catch him shrug. Lord, she envied his calm. Lately, it seemed whenever he was around, she had a hard time concentrating on anything but his broad shoulders. Firm lips. Rock-hard abs he unintentionally gifted her with glimpses of whenever the weather was warm enough for him to work in one of his tight, white undershirts. "Sure you're okay?"

"It's hot." Jess covered her obvious, unseemly thoughts by fanning her hand in front of her face. "Did you have to build such a huge fire?"

"No, but seeing how it's about fifteen degrees outside, I figured you and the girls might appreciate the heat."

Ha! Little did Gage know that whenever he was around, her internal heater did a fine job of keeping her hot!

TWO MONTHS PASSED, during which, much to her eldest daughter's dismay, Jess grew ever more appreciative of Gage's help. Even better was their easy, flirtatious camaraderie. With every womanly bone in her body, she sensed he wanted to explore an added dimension to their already growing friendship, but at the moment, that just wasn't possible.

In so many ways, he was a lifesaver, but just as she had feared, Lexie's attitude was worse than ever. Even at school, her teacher reported that she acted as if her cast was a license to whine—about everything. Jess knew the girl was still hurting, but she seemed to delight in making others hurt, as well. Not physically, but emotionally. The closer Ashley grew to Gage, the more Lexie seemed to resent him. She wanted him off the ranch, and never missed an opportunity to tell him.

Daffodil had safely given birth to an amazing painted colt. Word had spread how perfect his coat was, and Jess had already been made several enormous offers for the little guy.

Honey had fully recovered, and was maturing nicely. His accident seemed to have squelched some of his wandering ways. Or maybe it'd just been the rough winter weather keeping him close to the barn.

No additional trash had been dumped in the valley where Honey had nearly lost his life.

Aside from worrying about her eldest daughter, Jess hadn't been so at ease with her life in a long while. She'd like to believe that fact had little to do with Gage, but as she sat outside the girls' school, waiting to pick them up, she knew better.

All afternoon, she'd run errands in sloppy rain. Grocery store, feed store, pharmacy. The giddy, guilty pleasure she felt stemmed from the thought of getting back home to Gage and told her she was in over her head when it came to her feelings for him.

True to his word, he hadn't kissed her or so much as touched her again. The fact should've made her happy, but all it really did was drive her nuts.

Ashley ran toward the truck, pigtails flopping. For the moment, the rain had stopped, but the sky looked ready to spill again at any time.

"Hi, Mommy!" The second Ashley hopped onto the seat, she scooted closer for a kiss and hug. "I missed you."

"I missed you, too," Jess said, returning her daughter's affection.

"Look what I made!" She grabbed a rolled-up painting from her backpack. It was of a man and woman holding hands, with a little girl and a half-dozen horses standing alongside them. Their family? Was she starting to think of Gage as her father? But where was her sister?

Jess jumped when someone knocked on the driver's-side window. It was Lexie's teacher. Lexie was beside her, usual glower in place.

Jess rolled down the window. "Hi, Mrs. Franklin. Can I help you?"

"Actually," the thirtysomething teacher said, brown eyes somber, "I was wondering if you'd have a few minutes to talk?"

"Now?" That formerly happy feeling in Jess's stomach? Instantly gone. As if Ashley's picture hadn't given her enough to ponder, now this?

"If you have time."

Lexie shifted her weight from one foot to the other.

"Um, sure," Jess said. "Come on, Ash, I don't want you out here alone."

"What about me?" Lexie asked.

"You're coming, too." Trailing after the teacher, holding both girls' hands, transported Jess to junior high when she'd spent too much time in detention for talking.

A million years ago, Jess had attended the same elementary school, and the place still smelled the same. Like kid sweat and bubble gum and chalk dust with a hint of cafeteria meat loaf thrown in for good measure.

"Girls," Mrs. Franklin said, holding open her classroom door, "how about you two wait out here? We'll be right back."

Seated in a too-small chair at a table so short her

knees didn't even fit under, Jess asked, "Let's hear it. What's Lex done this time? Paste in your chair? Stabbing a boy with a pencil?"

The faint smile on Mrs. Franklin's face didn't come close to reaching her eyes. "I, ah, wish it were that simple. I've actually been meaning to speak with you for a while, but wanted this to be in person rather than over the phone."

Jess's heart stopped for a moment. Whatever the woman had to say, it couldn't be good.

"I don't even know where to begin," the teacher said, primly crossing her legs and smoothing her navy skirt over her knees.

"Please," Jess urged, "with afternoon chores ahead of me, jump right in. Whatever my daughter's done, I can handle it."

"That's just it…" The woman gazed out at the still-bustling school front. While other moms and their sons and daughters enjoyed afternoon hugs, Jess was on the verge of puking. "Mrs. Cummings, how well do you know the man who's been staying with you?"

"Gage?" Jess struggled to stay in her seat, let alone keep a civil tone. "He's an old family friend. Not that I knew him before he started work on the ranch, but my folks did. And Doc Matthews and his wife. All of them think very highly of Gage, and I've never seen anyone put in longer days' work."

"I understand you must respect him, or you'd have never welcomed him into your home, but—"

"Gage doesn't live in our house. Is that what Lexie told you?"

"Well, yes, but—"

"He lives in the bunkhouse. He takes meals with us, but that's all." Much to Jess's everlasting disappointment.

"Getting straight to the point, Lexie has told me on numerous occasions that this man is not only mean to her, but that he's responsible for breaking her arm. Now, knowing of Lexie's history, her emotional issues over losing her father, I wanted to come to you first with this information. But you have to know that if even a shred of what she's said is true, I'll have to report this man to proper authorities."

Anger didn't begin to describe the rage growing within Jess. How could Lexie do this? Gage had been amazing to her. Patient and kind and…had she already forgotten the covered wagon he'd made her? The way he'd carried her to his truck and into her doctor's office when she'd broken her arm? Jess had to clasp her knees to keep her hands from trembling.

"I appreciate the courtesy you've shown in coming to me first, Mrs. Franklin, but rest assured, with every fiber of my being, I promise you, Gage Moore has never—in any way—harmed my daughter. She broke her arm during the Christmas storm, by standing on top of an icy tire swing. I was there at the time. So was her sister."

"And Mr. Moore?" the teacher asked, now taking notes.

"He was there, too. Standing a good fifty feet away. Lexie had just smashed to smithereens a snowman he and Ashley had spent a good chunk of the afternoon working on. I'll be the first to admit Lexie resents Gage's presence on the ranch, but it's my belief that is because she thinks he's trying to take my husband's place."

"If you don't mind my asking," the woman gently asked, "is he?"

"No. No, of course not," Jess said with a firm shake

of her head. "He's a good friend to me and my youngest daughter. Nothing more. I can't imagine what's led Lexie to make such a cruel accusation, but her behavior has gotten to the point that I think she may need professional help."

Jotting additional notes, Mrs. Franklin said, "Sadly, if what you say is true, I have to agree."

JESS BIT HER TONGUE until after they got home. She kept right on biting through dinner, and cleaning up after dinner, and bathtime and even after tucking Ashley into bed. With Gage long since in the bunkhouse, however, Jess wasn't waiting a minute more.

"Lex," she said, careful not to tuck the covers too tightly around Lexie's cast, "do you know what Mrs. Franklin wanted to talk to me about?"

"No." She tugged her fuzzy pink blanket over her mouth. "How should I know?"

"Because you're the one who told her something that could get a very good friend of mine in a whole lot of trouble."

Lexie stayed quiet, scowl intense enough to have furrowed her eyebrows.

"The look on your face tells me you know exactly what you did. I also know all of this anger inside of you has to come out. Sweetie, we all miss your dad, but you can't go on like this. Being angry all the time. He wouldn't want you to be this way."

"How do you know?" Lexie said in a whispered taunt. "And what do you think Daddy would say about you kissing Gage? I saw you. I saw you, Mommy, kissing that man. I thought you loved Daddy? When he died, you told me and Ashley you'd always love him."

In movies, Jess had heard characters claim to be

physically ill from the depth of their emotional pain. Being a hardworking, practical woman, she'd never set much store in those kinds of things. But the blankness in her daughter's eyes brought her earlier nausea back tenfold. Anyone could see the girl was badly hurt, yet she didn't cry. Come to think of it, lately, she *never* cried.

Not since before Dwayne's death.

"Sweetheart," she said, cradling her girl, rocking her like she had when Lex had been a baby, "I will always love your father, but I have to go on—*we* have to go on."

"How can you say that?" Tearing herself free, she screamed, "I hate you! I hate Ashley! I hate Gage! I hate Grandma and Grandpa and Doc and Miz Martha! I hate all of you for forgetting my daddy!" Bolting for the door, she took off down the hall.

Jess made a futile attempt at chasing after her, but in the end, she took a seat on one of the bottom stairs, holding her head in her hands.

How had her life come to this? Just when things looked like they were turning around, Lexie was worse than ever. Did their meager health insurance even cover psychological care?

"Mommy?" At the top of the stairs stood Ashley, stuffed pink dino in hand. "I heard yelling."

"Everything's okay. Go on back to bed."

"I can't sleep. Can I get in your bed?"

"Sure," Jess said, too tired to fight her. Sleeping with her youngest was like sharing her bed with a twister. The girl was always tossing and turning and kicking. But that was okay. She had a feeling that tonight, she'd need all the company she could get.

Guiltily, who she really wanted to talk to was Gage, but obviously, that wouldn't work. Her brief fantasies of maybe starting a new life—a new family—with him were just that, fantasies. Because if Jess's conscience by chance did allow her to make a play for Gage, Lexie sure as hell wouldn't.

"THAT'S IT," GAGE SAID that night in front of the fire. The girls had long since gone to bed, and he and Jess had been mulling over their days. It was then she'd told him about her impromptu conference with Lexie's teacher. "No matter how much I love being on the ranch with you and Ashley, for Lexie's sake, I've got to go."

"But don't you see?" Jess said, leaning forward from her seat on the sofa's far corner. "That's what she wants. How is that going to help her? Gage, if it's not you she resents being on the ranch, it'll be the next person hired to help. And if there's one thing your being here has taught me, it's that I can't handle this place on my own. I was a fool for thinking I could."

"No," he said, itching to go to her. Hold her. Make everything all right. Instead, he held firm to his seat on the cold stone hearth. Even though a fire crackled, it was newly made, and not yet putting out adequate warmth. "You were doing the best you could. That's all anyone could ask of you—especially your Dwayne."

Eyes downcast, she whispered, "Thank you, for that."

"I mean it, Jess. I've never met anyone like you."

"I could say the same about you." She smiled, stomping his heart as effectively as a rogue bull.

"I'm going to call a child psychiatrist in the morning. Lexie's teacher gave me a few names of doctors specializing in grief. They're all at least a good hour or more away, but I think it'll be worth it, don't you?"

Sighing, rubbing his face with his hands, he said, "I

don't know what to believe. You have to know that if you think my leaving will magically cure your girl, then I'll gladly do it. Not that I'll be happy about it," he added with a faint smile, "but for her—for *you*—I'll go."

Chapter Eleven

"Are you sure?" Jess had been on the phone with the psychiatrist's receptionist for the past twenty minutes. The girls weren't yet home from school, and Gage was repairing a loose part of the barn roof. "Would you mind checking again?"

"I'm sorry, ma'am," the woman said, her voice distorted by the static in the connection, "but I've already checked your insurance information twice and Doctor Richardson's services aren't covered."

Jess's heart sank. "And how much did you say he charges per hour?"

"Two hundred and forty, which I know may seem like a lot, but if you'd like, we can work out a no-interest finance plan."

"Thank you," Jess said, "I'll, um, have to think about it, and get back to you."

"The doctor's schedule is awfully full. I'd recommend booking soon."

"Yes, yes, I will." Jess hung up, only to worry the inside of her lower lip. Okay, so great. What was she supposed to do now? She'd phoned every psychiatrist on the list, and they were all financially out of her reach. There was no way she could afford that kind of money.

Neither could her parents or Dwayne's. Lexie desperately needed more than Jess could give her, but this wasn't the way she'd get it.

"Get a hold of the shrink?" Gage bustled through the back door. The sky was gray, and the forecast was for snow flurries.

"He was all filled up," Jess said with forced gaiety.

"Did you try any of the others?" He removed his coat and hat. "Didn't Lexie's teacher give you three names of guys specializing in grief?"

"Yes, but their schedules were nuts. I'll call back in a week."

"Wouldn't it be better to at least get on a waiting list?"

"Gage," she warned, "whose daughter is she? I've got this handled."

"All right," he said, hands up in the universal sign of surrender, "just know I'm here if you need me."

LATE THAT AFTERNOON, Gage rubbed his weary eyes with his thumb and forefinger. All he'd wanted was to grab a quick shower and predinner nap. All he was going to get was more work.

Surveying the mess on his bed, Gage surmised that if Jess had her daughter's issues handled, then he was the damned Easter Bunny.

Someone—aka, Lexie—had written *Go Home* on his pillows with mustard. On the quilt was *I Hate You* in ketchup.

Sitting in the rocker in front of the woodstove, Gage stared into the fire. What was he supposed to do? No matter what Lexie believed, he was needed. Aside from when her eldest daughter was around, Jess had never seemed more relaxed. How she might have been back before her husband had died.

What Gage would give to have known her then, even though she had been married to another man. For all practical purposes, she was still off-limits, and he certainly wasn't in the market for romance. So why, then, did he crave that glimpse into the past? Maybe because if he had a good baseline to start from, he'd know how far he had to go to restore her—and her daughters'— former happiness.

He thought about grabbing Jess and making her see the damage Lexie had done, but changed his mind, choosing instead to go a different route.

Whistling his way into the house, acting as if he hadn't a care in the world, he made small talk with Jess and helped her peel potatoes. He helped Ashley color in her favorite dinosaur coloring book. He then excused himself to go to the restroom, only to instead find Lexie in the office, playing on the computer.

Pulling a chair up alongside her, he eased back, resting his right ankle on his knee. "Do anything special after school today?"

"No." She didn't so much as glance his way.

"Funny, because I really got a kick out of the practical joke someone played on me. The masterpiece wasn't signed, but I figured with that much raw talent on display, the artist could've only been you."

She continued with Barbie's on-screen makeover.

"I also truly enjoyed the choice of medium. Do you know what that is? The word *medium?*"

"No."

"I'll be happy to educate you. It's the material an artist uses to complete his or her works. Now, most artists use oil or watercolor paint, but this artist used ketchup and mustard. Isn't that creative?"

She glared at the computer screen.

Planting both feet square on the hardwood floor, he rested his elbows on his knees. "Let's cut the crap, shall we? You and I both know you're the one who made that mess in the bunkhouse." Softening his voice, he continued with, "I know somewhere behind that eternal frown of yours is an amazing heart, Lexie. And I also know how much you love your mom. Whether you believe me or not, your behavior is breaking her heart. So, as a favor to her, I'm not going to tell her about this creative streak of yours and you're not, either. Instead, you're going to find me a clean quilt, and a couple of pillowcases, and you're going to wash and fold the ones you messed up. Understand?"

"No." She still glared, but this time at her hands, which she held tightly clasped in her lap.

"Great." He patted her back. "Thanks for being so sweet to your mother. I'm sure she'd be proud."

"Wow," Jess said, drying her hands on a dishrag after dinner. She and Gage had just finished the dishes while the girls tackled the rest of their homework. "What's up with that?"

In the laundry room, Lexie was shoving sheets into the washer, followed by a quilt.

"Um, not that I don't appreciate your trying to help," she said, kissing her daughter's head, "but maybe you should start off with a smaller load?"

"Sure, Mom. I just want to help." She beamed not at Jess, but somewhere behind her. Jess turned around to find Gage, but why would Lexie be smiling at him? "Can you show me what to do?"

"I-I'd be happy to. Gage, would you mind finishing up here?"

"Not a bit," he said. "You gals carry on."

A couple of hours later, Jess and Gage sat watching a romantic comedy DVD. Lexie was upstairs playing with her dolls and Ashley was acting very grown-up, yakking with a school friend on the kitchen phone.

"What'd you think of Lexie volunteering to help with chores?" she asked during a lull in the action.

"Pretty amazing." He grabbed a handful of the buttered popcorn they'd been sharing. "If I hadn't seen it with my own eyes, I wouldn't have believed it."

"What do you think got into her?"

"Beats me, but I like it."

She dived into the popcorn bowl, too, inadvertently grazing Gage's hand. Shocked by the momentary contact, not wanting him to realize how badly she wanted his touch, she drew back sharply.

"You all right?" He eyed her.

"Sure." She crammed a handful of popcorn into her mouth. After swallowing, she asked, "Why wouldn't I be?"

He shrugged. "You seem jumpy."

"Nope." She hoped the smile she sent his way wasn't too forced.

"Good." His smile was amazing. Brimming with strong, white teeth, and extending all the way to heart-melting chocolate-brown eyes. He reached out, extending his pinkie as if he'd meant to brush it along hers, but Ashley bounded into the room, and the spell was broken as he jerked his hand away.

"Mommy?"

"Yes, ma'am."

"Can we bake cookies?" The girl bounced with her question, pigtails flopping. "Angela's mom just made chocolate chip."

"Sweetie, it's kind of your bedtime."

"Pleeeeease?"

"Nope." Jess held firm.

Ashley crossed her arms and thrust out her chin. "The only way I'm sleeping is if we bake cookies or if Mister Gage tucks me in."

"Hmm…" Jess hazarded a glance toward Gage. What would he think about suddenly being thrust into a parental role? "I know I'm not baking cookies, but I'd be happy to tuck you in."

"So would I," Gage said, ruffling the girl's hair. "How about me and your mom tuck you in together?"

"Yeah!" Ashley said, jumping up and down. "That'll be fun." She grabbed Gage's hand, then Jess's, dragging them both off the sofa and up the stairs. In her room, bouncing on the bed, Ashley didn't look anywhere near sleeping.

"How about taking it down a notch, sweetie?" Snatching her girl around her waist, Jess tugged her into the bed. Ashley had long since changed into green, dino-patterned flannel jammies, so when she flopped onto her back, Jess seized the opportunity to whip back the covers, get the girl comfy, then tuck her in up to her chin.

"I want Mister Gage to tuck, too."

"Ah, sure," Gage said, easing past Jess to give a few obligatory swipes at Ashley's green down blanket.

Out of nowhere, Ashley sat up, tossing her arms around Gage's neck before kissing his stubbled cheek. "I love you, Mister Gage. Are you going to marry Mommy and be my new dad?"

"Um…" Gage hadn't been this stunned since the last time he'd been bucked off a ride. Holy crap, had this girl seriously just invited him into the family? Unlatching Ashley's chubby hands from his neck, then backing away to perch on the edge of the bed, he said, "Gee, Tater Tot, I, ah, haven't given it much thought. I mean, I'd love to be your dad, but I, ah, think that, um, you already have one. He might not be with you at the house, but he'll always be in here." He patted his chest.

"What Mister Gage is trying to say," Jess offered, "is that it's complicated to—"

"Get married," Gage interjected. "Lots of papers."

"Uh-huh," Jess said with a big nod. "Lots—*tons* of papers."

"And food," Gage explained. "Tons—gobs of food involved in a wedding. There's no way we could ever possibly come up with that much."

"Oh." Ashley froze, taking it all in. "If I make bologna sandwiches, would that help?"

"WHAT WAS THAT?" Jess asked in the kitchen after having finally gotten Ashley settled down, and Lexie at least in her bed—there was no guarantee she was sleeping. "I mean, did my kid just ask you to marry her? I mean, *us?*" If her cheeks grew any hotter, they'd blister.

"She's confused," Gage said, head in the fridge.

"What are you looking for?"

"Pretty much anything." He emerged with a jar of green olives, unscrewed the lid and popped about three into his mouth. "It's been kind of a strange night."

"You think?" She held out her hand. "Give me those. I need a few, too."

"You know what would really hit the spot?"

In unison, both grinning, they said, "Chocolate chip cookies."

Forty minutes later, flour-coated and weary, they met up at the kitchen table, a plate of fresh-baked cookies between them, and each with a tall tumbler of cold milk.

"Let's toast," he said, raising his glass. "To kids. God love 'em, they never make life dull."

"To kids," she said, clinking her glass to his.

After an awkward silence, during which they both downed at least three cookies apiece, Gage said, "One thing you should know, Jess…we've made light of Ashley's question up there, but *if* things were different in my own life, I'd be proud to marry you."

"*If* things were different?" She nearly choked on her latest bite. "Talk about romantic."

"You know what I mean."

Yes, she did, but that didn't make it any easier to stomach. The man she fantasized about morning, noon and night obviously didn't care about her beyond the sense of obligation that kept him working on the ranch.

"Jess…I didn't mean that in a bad way. You know I think the world of you and the girls, and—"

"Don't." Gaze downcast, she pressed her hand to the base of her throat, regretting the whole cookie thing, as acid indigestion now burned a hole in her throat. "Please, just don't. We both know what we are to each other. We should leave it at that."

"Would you mind defining *that* for me?"

"Pardon?" Jess pressed her fingertips to her throbbing forehead. "What aren't you clear on?"

"I guess the part where we both supposedly know what's going on between us, because truthfully, I've never in my life had a *friend* I so badly want to kiss."

Jess slid her hands down to cover her gaping mouth.

"Not that I'm *going* to kiss you, because we both know that wouldn't be wise."

Yes, it would! Only just now did Jess realize how

badly she wanted to kiss Gage. But like him, she understood the attraction simmering between them couldn't
be explored. She needed to put Lexie first.

"Jess?"

"Uh-huh?" He'd slid his chair sideways, rested his
hands on her knees. His radiating heat had become a
living thing. Pulsing and vibrating between them. To
say she *just* wanted to kiss him was the understatement
of the century. Her breasts even ached for his touch.

"Tell me what you're thinking."

Because she couldn't—mustn't—she held her lips
clamped tightly and merely shook her head.

"Please," he coaxed, rubbing her inner thighs with
his thumbs. Even through jeans, his touch burned red-
hot. "Honestly…" Glancing down, then up, he pierced
her with a painfully direct gaze. "I'd feel much better
knowing I'm not alone in this…this struggle keeping
my hands to myself."

Licking her lips, she nodded. It'd been so long since
she'd been touched by a man that her body hummed for
Gage's attention. As corny as it sounded, she craved him
like air.

"Am I, Jess? Alone?"

Pulse thundering in her ears, she whispered, "No."

After a sharp exhale, he leaned forward, resting his
forehead against hers. Their breaths mingled. Her stomach fluttered.

"Do you feel better?" she asked.

With a barely perceptible shake of his head, he said,
"Nowhere close."

Chapter Twelve

Gage's mood should've been lightened by the note on his freshly made bed. *I still hate you!* had been written in pink marker on a sheet of pink notebook paper, then set atop his favorite down pillow. Trouble was, as satisfying as this infinitesimal progress was with Lexie, it didn't matter. Judging by the talk they'd just shared, he and Jess were on the same page when it came to the two of them. A blank page. Meaning nothing would ever come of their attraction.

A good thing, right? After all, even if Jess had confessed her undying devotion, and Lexie enjoyed his company as much as her little sister, there were still his own issues between them. The fact that he wasn't anywhere near good enough for her or her girls.

In the morning, not yet ready to face Jess after their late-night confessions, he rode fences. The day was fine for early March. Balmy. The air grassy-sweet, teasing of spring.

A dust cloud rose on the road, preceded by the girls' school bus.

Eyes closed, he envisioned Jess standing alongside the road, waving the girls on their way. Her hair would be pulled into a loose ponytail, stray curls floating on the soft morning breeze. In a perfect world, he'd be alongside her, his arm loose around her waist. Only it wasn't a perfect world, but a crappy one, apparently destined to get worse before it got better.

When Gage reached the valley where Honey had been hurt, he found more trash than ever. This time, the carcass of a rusty, pale blue VW Bug had been dumped— no plates left on it—along with a couple dozen crates of oily auto parts. Boxes and boxes of busted, home-made canned goods, swarming with flies. He searched through it all for any names, but again, came up empty.

By the time he headed back to the house, the sun was nearly midsky. The whole time he'd been gone, he'd searched for the right thing to say. Something casual, yet not flippant. Thoughtful, yet not sappy. He didn't want Jess thinking he hadn't cared about their talk, but he also didn't want to seem as if he were dwelling on it. Like he was, but—

"It's about time you showed up," Jess said in the center of the yard, hands on her hips. "Where have you been?"

"Riding fences."

"That's a cowboy cliché if I've ever heard one."

Tipping his hat, he quipped with a slow grin, "Happens to be true. Now, what's the problem?"

"The kitchen sink's clogged."

Eyebrows raised, he asked, "And Miss Independent is consulting me about this, why?" He climbed off his horse, taking the reins to lead her into the barn.

"Granted, I may have been a little standoffish at first when it came to you helping out around here, but—"

"A little?" He coughed.

"Okay, a *lot*," she admitted, "so does that mean you'll fix the sink? Because it's really greasy and icky and—"

"I'll do it," he said. "Just let me brush down Henrietta, and I'll be right in."

"Thank you." She crushed him in a hug that didn't last nearly long enough, then was off, shouting over her shoulder, "Want me to get a few tools for you?"

"No, thanks. I've got it handled."

She shot him one last smile before going inside. Oh, he might have the clog handled, but when it came to his feelings for Jess, he didn't have a clue what to do.

"THAT WAS AWFULLY handy of you to fix the sink," Georgia said that night over dinner. "Harold, here, is hopeless when it comes to fixing anything around the house." Jess had called her parents over to help celebrate Ashley's having been named Student of the Month at her school.

"Watch it," Harold complained. "I have been known to change a lightbulb every now and then."

"Mostly *then,*" Georgia said with a snort.

"Gramma?" Ashley asked from across the table. She leaned to her side, holding out a chunk of meat loaf for Taffy, who snapped it up.

"Yes, sweetie?"

"What's handy?"

"Let me get this," Harold offered. "*Handy* is when a good man like Gage, here, takes care of his family. And for looking after our girls, that's what you've become. A very good man, and a member of our family."

"Hear! Hear!" Georgia said, raising her iced tea.

"Thanks for the kind words," Gage said, "but all I did was unclog a sink. Anybody could've done it."

"Anybody but your husband, right, Georgia?" Harold laughed. Everyone else joined in with him.

Jess sat back, arms relaxed at her sides. The night

had been almost perfect except for Lexie, who wore her customary scowl. Her father had complimented her spaghetti and salad with homemade Caesar dressing. And her mother had loved the freshly baked caramel pecan rolls, as did her daughters. As for Gage, judging by the three heaping platefuls he'd consumed of everything, he'd taken pleasure in it all. Which made Jess inordinately happy. Was it wrong of her to take pleasure in watching him eat? To allow her eyes to linger over the play of his muscles in his hands? The way his eyes closed the slightest bit while savoring a bite?

"Jess? Honey? What do you think?" Georgia elbowed her. "Have you heard a word I've said?"

Averting her eyes from Gage, fearing she'd been staring, Jess cleared her throat. "Sorry. I'm tired. You caught me daydreaming."

"But it's night, Mommy," Ashley was all too happy to point out.

"That it is," Jess said with a laugh. "Ready for bed?"

"No way! Grandpa promised to play dinosaurs with me."

"Then I guess I'd better get on it," Harold said, pushing back his chair. "Ready?" He held out his hand and Ashley took it.

"Does my heart good, seeing those two together," Georgia said.

"Ashley's stupid." Lexie didn't bother looking up from her second pecan roll.

"Lex," Jess scolded.

"You can be mad at me," the girl said, "I don't care. And Gage isn't our family. He isn't anybody and I hate him!"

"Lexie Margaret Cummings," Georgia said, pounding her palms on the table. "What's wrong with you?"

The girl's answer was to take off running for the stairs.

The dog bolted after her.

Groaning, elbows on the table, Gage rested his head in his hands. "I'm so sorry. All of this is my fault."

"How?" Jess stood, grabbing dirtied plates from the table. "She was like this before you came, and she'll no doubt be like this after you leave."

"So I'm leaving?" Gage asked.

"Of course not," Georgia said, standing to help clear the table.

Gage joined in on the work. "It might be best. For everyone."

"Not Jess. Or Ashley." Stepping up behind him, Georgia planted her hands on his shoulders. "Or, for that matter, Lexie. Did it ever occur to you, Gage, that she's testing you? Throwing out every nasty trick in her book just to see how much you'll take before leaving her just like her father?"

"Dwayne died," Gage said. "Don't you think that's a little different?"

"Do you?" Georgia gave him a hug. "Jess? What do you think?"

"You know what, Mom?" Hands braced on the counter's edge, she sighed. "At the moment, I'm too tired to think. I just want to sleep and sleep and wake up with my life back the way it was."

"You know that can't happen, don't you?"

Lips pressed tight, Jess held back from launching a string of obscenities at her well-meaning mother. What the hell kind of question was that? Honestly, who in the world would know better than her just what a hopeless situation she was in?

"Jess?" Georgia coaxed.

"Oh, for goodness' sake, Mom, leave it alone."

"How can I leave it alone when I love you? I worry about you. Can't you see that? That's why your father and I were so happy to see Gage come. You need a man around to—"

"No, Mom," Jess said more roughly than she intended, but was unable to control the depth of her emotion. "I don't need a man around—or anyone. Yes, I'll be the first to admit that it's been wonderful having Gage here, but I've known from the start that he wouldn't stay. He's got his own life to lead. Why would he stick around here?"

"Come on, Jess…" Gage was at her side, hovering near as if he wanted to comfort her, but was afraid. "I'm not going anywhere, okay? Promise, I'll stay as long as you like."

"Stop it." Jess held her hands over her ears. "Both of you." Realizing she must seem as childish as her eldest daughter, Jess lowered her hands, but not her level of frustration. "Mom, I know you mean well, but please, stay out of it."

Her mother's eyes widened. "So then I do at least have hope of you one day getting remarried?"

"Jeez, Mom, what's your problem?" Jess groaned in frustration. "Why can't you just be happy with me living my life the way I want?"

"Because you forget… I've known you your whole life, and for the past year—up until Gage came— you've done nothing but work and sleep. Now, the dark circles under your eyes are gone." Her mother clutched Jess's hands, tipping them palms-up. "Your hands used to be a fright. Nails torn. Palms stained from those awful old work gloves. They don't even fit."

"That's because they were Dwayne's, all right? They're all I have left of him."

"Bull," Georgia said, drying tears from Jess's cheeks with the soft pads of her thumbs. "You have this ranch, and two beautiful little girls, and a heart that's too full to give up on life."

Jess hadn't given up on life, just the man who might have transformed her black-and-white world to color. The man, currently standing across the room with his arms crossed, who looked as if he were dying to bolt. And if he was, who could blame him? Crazy mom, crazy kid, Jess was surrounded by crazies—biggest of all, herself, for harboring secret fantasies that she and Gage and the girls could live happily ever after.

MUCKING OUT STALLS the next morning after the girls were already off for school, Gage noticed Jess wasn't her usual chatty self. "You're not still brooding over all that stuff your mom said, are you?"

"I don't brood," she said, fire practically flashing from her pretty blue eyes. "For the record, I'm in a perfectly fine mood."

"I can tell." His smile was lost on her as she didn't even bother looking up from her chore. "Want to talk about it?"

"If I wanted to talk, I would. But I don't, so I'm not."

"Ouch." With the weather having been so fine, all of the horses were out to pasture, and the breeze sweeping through the barn carried with it the honeyed scent of daffodils blooming all over the front yard. The grass already needed a mowing, as in spots it was overgrown, but Jess had asked him to hold off. Because he was head over heels when it came to the woman, he bowed to her wish. Now he understood why she'd made the request. "Your flowers are pretty. I see why you didn't want me mowing them down."

She graced him with an unladylike grunt.

Okay… "How'd there ever get to be so many? Was there an old homestead before the house that's there now?"

"Yep." She pitched her latest load of manure into the wheelbarrow.

He whistled. "Seeing how my attempts at conversing have died horrible deaths, how about we get straight to the point, and you tell me what I did to make you not even look at me, let alone talk."

Still, silence.

"I'm going to take a wild stab here, and say your current mood has something to do with last night. I would've figured that out of anyone, you'd be upset with your mom, but apparently I was wrong. It's me you're wanting to lash with a roll of barbed wire. My only question is…why?"

"Don't you ever shut up?" She spun around to face him, stabbing her pitchfork in the wheelbarrow's manure pile. "Good Lord, almighty, I've had chatty women friends as annoying as you, but never a man. Can't you just leave well enough alone?"

"Oh, I'd be happy to," he said after a sarcastic snort. "Only trouble is, I don't think we're in a *well enough* situation." Stabbing his pitchfork alongside hers, then removing his leather work gloves only to tuck them in his back pocket, he said, "What we seem to have here is a genuine hornets' nest. Complete with a queen bee."

"Bees and hornets don't mix." She turned her back on him, heading for the feed.

All right, if that was the way she wanted to play it…

It took only a second to cross to her part of the barn. Another to pin her, lean in close, rest his hands on either side of her shoulders, his palms flattened on the coarse, wood-planked wall. "Listen up, Miss Sassy Pants. I take enough verbal abuse from your oldest munchkin. I'm not accustomed to taking it from her momma, too."

"Let me go," she said from between clenched teeth. Her halfhearted squirming only turned him on.

"I will," he said, "just as soon as you fill me in on what I did wrong."

"For starters," she said, "last night you just stood there like a big old box of bricks. Why couldn't you have said something—anything—in my defense?"

"Defense of what? You're all the time reminding me, Jess, how you're a grown woman, fully capable of taking care of yourself."

Fingers splayed, pressing against his chest, she blurted, "You wanna know why I'm so all-fired furious with you?"

"Hell, yes. Why else do you think we're standing here?"

"Last night, when Mom made that quip about me one day remarrying, I looked behind her to find you, studying my oven mitts as if you'd just discovered a fascinating new species of bull."

"What can I say?" he asked, lead lining his stomach. "The fabric pattern is real pretty."

"Grrrr…" She pushed harder against him, but he was a rock, and they weren't going anywhere until this was settled.

"In all seriousness, Jess, what would you have wanted me to do?"

"Oh—we're going to be serious?"

"Dammit, woman, stop pussyfooting around, and tell me what's on your mind."

Her eyes were huge and wet. She looked away,

clenching his worn, white T-shirt. "Nothing, okay. Let's just forget it."

"Sure?" With the thumb of one hand, he brushed the apple of her cheek.

She nodded.

"Then we're cool?" Could she tell he was more than a little relieved? Because for a minute there, her wistful expression had scared him. Like she may have wanted more than he might ever be ready to give.

He kissed her. Nothing fancy. Just a quiet pressing of his lips against hers that turned his very soul inside out. What was wrong with him that he couldn't put aside the past to make way for an amazing future with Jess and her girls?

An image of his sister flashed before his mind's eye. The look on her face as she'd lain on that damned ambulance gurney dying. The look that'd silently asked, *Why did you do this to me?*

"Stop it," Jess said, voice raspy with unshed tears. "Don't you dare kiss me so sweetly, when I know that ultimately, you'll break my heart. Gage Moore, you're nothing but a stereotypical, garden-variety love-'em-and-leave-'em cowboy. Out for nothing but your own good time."

"Would you listen to yourself? Do you honestly think the past few months have been a barrel of freakin' monkeys? I've worked my tail off—for you, Jess. All for *you.* Hell, sometimes I'm afraid to drift off to sleep at night, for fear of knowing you were only a dream, but then—" Abruptly straightening, he shoved his hands in his pockets, and walked away. Kept right on walking out into the yard, praying for the warm, spring sun to whitewash his sins.

"Don't you dare walk away from me," Jess cried,

chasing after him like a fired-up hen. "As much as I hate to admit it, I'm afraid I'm falling for you, Gage Moore. I'm not proud of the fact, but there it is, out in broad daylight for all to see. Now, judging by that kiss, you're not entirely repulsed by me, so why can't you just—"

"What, Jess? You want me to do this?" Cupping her cheeks, he kissed her proper. The way a man who loved a woman should. Only just now did he realize how much he'd grown to love this woman, which would make leaving her all the harder.

"Stop it," she said, pushing him away, only to pull him back, returning his kiss and then some. "I despise you. I thought I had everything all figured out, but then you came along and turned my life upside down."

"Ditto." He kissed the tip of her nose and her eyelids and her chin. He hurt from wanting her.

Kissing him harder, teasing him with a sexy stroke of her tongue, she pressed tight against him, leaving no doubt in his mind as to the fact that he wasn't alone in his needs.

"Make love to me," she said, blue eyes sparkling, chin raised.

Yes. Oh, hell, yes.

Deepening their kiss, he slid his rough hands under her shirt, sampling her velvety abdomen. Higher still, he found her satin bra, helping himself to the pliant warmth inside. Her nipple puckered beneath his palm, then he quickly withdrew his hand.

She groaned and arched her head back. But her expression wasn't one of pleasure, it was one of pain.

"What's the matter?" he asked.

"N-nothing," she said in that halting way he'd learned was an indicator of everything being wrong.

"Then why do you look ready to burst into tears?"

"I-I'm not."

He groaned. *Why?* Why had his momma raised him to be a gentleman? Why couldn't he be like so many of the jerks he rode with? Content with one-night stands? Tickled proverbial pink being the love-'em-and-leave-'em type Jess had already accused him of being.

"Please don't make me beg," she said with a soft, guttural mew. "It's been so long, and… I—I never planned on feeling this way, but…"

"Jess…" Forehead against hers, warm exhalations lingering between them, he said, "I'd give anything to lift you into my arms and carry you straight to bed."

"Then why won't you?" Her rejected expression ripped him in two.

"Because, baby, it wouldn't do either of us any good. I've got issues that need working out. You've said yourself that because of Lexie things would never work out between us, and I refuse to be *that* guy."

"What guy?"

He took her hand, caressing it. "The one who breaks your beautiful heart."

Chapter Thirteen

"You still here?" Lexie asked Gage on her way to grab an after-school snack from the fridge.

"'Fraid so, princess." Jess glanced his way in time to catch him wink.

Lexie stuck out her tongue.

Jess wanted to stay mad at him for denying her, but how could she when he'd been right? She hadn't been raised to go around throwing herself at men. But then Gage wasn't any old man, and it wasn't as if she'd picked him up at some bar, only to proposition him a few hours later. They'd shared time. He'd dried her tears. And she supposed she should be grateful to him for saving her from herself. Only she wasn't. Inside, she seethed over the fact that despite his rejection, her body still hummed with attraction.

"What's for dinner?" Lexie asked Jess.

"Pork chops."

"Again?" The girl made a face. "Why can't we have steak?"

"Maybe because it's too expensive," Jess reasoned, taking the chops from the freezer to thaw.

"But—"

"Mom! Gage!" Ashley burst through the back door. "Honey's missing!"

Gage glanced up from his second PB and J. "I'm sure he's somewhere close, Ash. Did you check around the south paddock?"

"Uh-huh," she said, still out of breath. "But he's not there. Buttercup's not, either."

"Hell," Gage mumbled so that only Jess could hear. "Guess I'd better go chase him down."

"Want me to come?" she asked.

"Nah. He's no doubt in the next pasture, chasing butterflies. Be right back." Snatching his hat from the top of the dryer, he headed out the same door through which Ashley had come running in.

"Can I go?" the little girl asked.

"How about you help your mom with supper? Then, when me and Honey and Buttercup get back, you can help with afternoon chores."

"'Kay," she said, squeezing him in a hug. "Come back soon."

"I will, Tater Tot."

"See you, Lex," Gage called out, his smile crinkling the corners of his eyes.

"My name's Lex-*eeeeeeee!*"

"I know," he said, dropping his hat on his head, treating her eldest daughter to the rogue's wink Jess had so grown to love.

GAGE RODE FOR A good hour, but still saw no sign of Honey or his mom. Along with the setting sun came a north wind that chilled him to his bones, but still, he kept riding.

Stomach heavy, he prayed the colt hadn't reverted to his bad-boy ways. Just in case, though, he clucked his tongue, angling his mount toward the trash-filled valley where Honey had last found trouble.

"Hi-yah," he called with a snap of the reigns, urging the mare into a hard run.

Fifteen minutes later, he'd reached the dump, only to have his worst fears confirmed. Honey was stretched out on his side, eyes wide and breathing labored. His stomach was distended. With a soft neigh, Buttercup nuzzled her colt.

As to what had caused the horse's discomfort, the evidence surrounded Gage. Canned goods packed in glass jars were strewn all around the colt. Sticky sweet, dripping with syrupy shattered glass.

Gage reached into his rear pocket for his cell, only to find it not there. Dammit. He'd taken it out while stripping for the cold shower Jess's curves had forced him into.

Great. Now what?

Kneeling beside the rasping colt, pulse raging, Gage tried lifting Honey, but it was no use. He was too big.

Buttercup snorted, nuzzling her baby.

"It's all right," Gage said, rising, rubbing her nose. "I'll bring help."

The return trip took an eternity, even though Gage rode his mare for all she was worth.

Riding straight up to the back door, it occurred to him that for the girls' sake, he should downplay the situation's urgency, but for Honey's sake, he rejected the idea.

Inside, he found Jess at the stove. Ashley and Lexie sat at the table, doing homework.

"Gage?" Jess turned to him. "What—"

"No time," he said. "Honey's done it again. Jess, call Doc. Tell him to meet us at the dump. Lex, I need you to take off Henrietta's saddle and blanket. Brush her down good. Give her extra oats. I had to ride her hard."

"O-okay," the girl said, for once, not giving him any lip.

"Is Honey going to die?" Ashley asked.

"I don't know, Tater Tot." The girl's eyes were wide, and her lower lip trembled. Pulling her into a hug, he said, "Once Doc gets here, we'll do all we can to help Honey feel better."

"Promise?"

"Sweetie," Gage said, "I wish I could, but I can't make that kind of guarantee."

"Mommy…" Ashley looked to Jess, but she was already on the phone.

"I'm going to go," Gage whispered to her, thumbing toward the door.

She shook her head, covered the mouthpiece of the phone. "I'm going with you."

"No. Stay here. The girls need you."

Slowly hanging up the phone, fumbling to fit it back into the stand, she nodded, pulling Ashley against her. "You're right. Hurry back."

Not giving a damn whether it was proper or not, he kissed the top of Ashley's head, then Jess's lips. "I'll bring him back safe, all right?"

Jess nodded.

"You have your phone?"

"I'll grab it when I get my truck keys."

"Call me. Call the second you get a feel for…"

Kissing her again, he made one promise he could keep. "I will."

TIME. IT WAS A FUNNY THING. The way sometimes an hour passed so fast, you wondered if it'd ever really happened at all. Then there were other hours, where each minute—each individual tick of the clock—was a long, drawn-out affair.

"Mommy?" Ashley looked up from the *Get Well* picture she'd been drawing for Honey.

"Yes, hon?"

"Do you think the phone rang already and we didn't hear it?"

"Don't be a dork," Lexie snapped.

"Tell you what," Jess said, ignoring her smart-mouthed eldest child, "how about you grab my cell phone from my purse and then call the house phone. That way, we'll for sure know."

"Okay." Ashley raced off for Jess's purse.

"Lexie," Jess asked, "what goes through your mind to always be so mean?"

The girl shrugged.

"No, I'd really be interested in knowing. Here, one of our favorite horses is hurting, yet just this once, you can't even manage to keep a civil tongue."

Head resting on folded arms, Lexie said, "I don't even know what that means."

Exasperated, Jess stood, shoulders aching from the strain of yet one more thing going wrong. Why, *why* couldn't this day freakin' end?

The phone rang, piercing the kitchen's tense silence to the point that even though Jess had been expecting Ashley's call, she'd still been startled. "Okay, sweetie!" she sang out. "The phone works."

"But, Mommy…" Ashley held up Jess's purse. "I haven't even found your phone."

Jess lurched to pick up. "Gage?"

"No, pumpkin, it's Mom." Jess's heart sank. "Rose

Crandolph says Honey's hurt again. Any word on how he's doing?"

Sighing, Jess rubbed her forehead. Rose was Doc's nosy neighbor. Mighty nice of her to spread this news. "Mom, I'm actually waiting for an update, so I'll have to let you go."

"But what happened?"

"Mom, I'm sorry, but I just don't know. Honey went missing this afternoon, and Gage found him and Buttercup in the valley where there's been all that dumping."

"Oh, no. I hate to hear that. How're the girls?"

"About as well as can be expected." Jess bit her lower lip to keep her tone from sounding too impatient. "I know you're as worried as we are, Mom, but I have to go in case Gage calls."

"Let me know as soon as you hear anything."

"I will." After disconnecting, Jess set the phone back on the charger, only to jump when it rang again. Hand to her racing heart, she answered, "Mom?"

"Gage. Listen, Jess…" He sighed. "There's no easy way to say this, so I'm just going to come right out with it. I'm with Doc down at the clinic and it looks bad. You might want to bring the girls so they can say their goodbyes."

IT'D BEEN A WHILE since Gage could remember having felt so helpless. The last time had been at his sister's side during her final moments, knowing there wasn't a damned thing he could do. Feeling like half a man because he'd been the cause of it.

Now, under the harsh fluorescent lights of Doc's big animal clinic, with Jess and the girls teary, Gage rammed his hands in his pockets, cursing a God who saw fit to so casually dole out so much pain. This family had already lost its lifeblood in losing Dwayne. How much more could they take?

Doc had done X-rays and tests on Honey to find that he'd ingested so much glass, he was not only suffering from food poisoning, but also massive internal bleeding. To save the creature from suffering, he advised putting him to sleep, but Gage had asked Doc to hold off until Jess and the girls arrived. They'd never gotten to say goodbye to their father. They should at least have the opportunity for one of their best friends.

"I—I love you, Honey," Ashley wailed, clinging to Jess's side.

"Please, don't die," Lexie said, her cheek to the colt's. His big brown eyes shone. *"Please…"*

Honey heaved a deep sigh and shuddered.

"Honey!" Lexie cried. *"Please!"*

It was too late for begging. The scrappy colt was gone.

"Nooo…" Lexie cried, sobbing her pain into Honey's mane.

Ashley started in with heartbreaking tears.

Gage wanted to go to her—to all of them. But what could he say?

Doc had been standing a polite distance away, but he now stepped forward, wrapping his arms around Jess, who didn't cry, but just stood there, eyes red-rimmed and watery, shoulders slumped while hugging her girl. "God has his reasons," the old man said.

"What God?" Jess asked with a sarcastic laugh.

"Don't…" Doc rubbed Jess's back. "You've already survived so much. Don't let this be the defining moment in your life where you choose to give up."

"I hate you!" Lexie thundered at Doc. "You just *let* Honey die! Why didn't you do something?"

"Lex…" Doc turned to her. "In my line of business, you can't always—"

"Shut up! I hate you!" The girl took off running for the clinic's front door.

"I should go after her," Jess said over Ashley's sobs.

"Let me…" Gage was already on his way.

"But she can't stand you," Jess argued.

Hands still in his pockets, he said, "Is there anyone the girl does like?"

Outside, now that the north wind had died down, the spring night was almost pleasant. The air was deliciously laced with the scent from someone's first grilled meal of the season. Off in a nearby ditch, spring peepers belted out a tune. Farther down the street, three boys laughed, chasing each other with flashlights.

The normalcy of it all felt wrong.

Couldn't everyone see there'd been a tragedy down here? Couldn't they have the decency to at least pretend to be as miserable as all of them?

Gage found Lexie seated in the bed of her mom's white pickup. She hugged her knees to her chest, staring straight ahead.

"Your mother's worried about you," he said, using the rear tire as a step to hop up and join her.

"I don't care. I hate her, too."

He sat beside her, stretching out his legs, crossing them at the ankles. "Not that it's any of my business, but what happens when you run out of folks to hate?"

"Go away. I hate you, too."

"That's a given," he said with a sad chuckle. "But you wanna know something funny?"

"No."

"Lately, I've kind of started liking you. You've got spunk. Just like a lot of the bull riders I know. They don't take crap from anyone—least of all some rowdy bull. I suspect you'll grow up to be the same." He gave her a sideways nudge, hoping—praying—for something in return. But all she had in her was a hollow-eyed stare.

"Lex…"

"My name's *Lex-eeeee.*"

"Sorry. *Lex-eeeeee…*" He took a deep breath, not sure he wanted to go down this particular road, but really had nowhere else to go. "I know you think no one understands the kind of pain you went through in losing your dad, and now, Honey, but I do."

She kept on staring straight ahead.

"Not too long ago, my sister died. I loved her like crazy. Growing up, we were best friends. In some ways, you remind me of her. The way you've got a few freckles on the tip of your nose. The way you sneak cookies when you think no one's watching."

"What's the matter with you?" she asked. "Are you some kind of spy?"

"Nope. But when I'm also sneaking cookies, I can't help but notice I've got competition."

"Why won't you leave me alone?"

Good question. Could the answer be that no matter how much grief this spitfire had doled out, he'd somehow managed to fall for her, as well as her mom and sister? "Truth is…I love you, Tater Tot. I'm worried about you."

"Don't worry." She pushed herself up.

He pushed her back down, only just now realizing that while he'd been much too late to have made a difference in his sister's life, he wasn't too late for Lexie.

Hell, he didn't know if he could help her or not, but he sure planned on trying.

"Oh," he said with a sarcastic laugh, "I'm going to worry. And like it or not, you're going to listen. Know what I think you're really saying every time you tell someone you hate them?"

Stone-eyed silence.

"Great. I'm so glad you're interested." He gave her another nudge. "I think you're saying you're scared. And that it's easier for you to shut yourself off from everyone than to let them in. Because if you let them in, you might lose them—like you did your dad. And that hurts too bad to even begin to deal with."

With a sideways glance, he noticed the girl's lower lip had begun to tremble. She'd contorted her feet around so that one landed atop the other. With everything in her, was she fighting to hold back tears?

"I also think that losing Honey hurts so bad, you can't even begin to describe how awful you feel. Like if you ever love anyone or anything again, and they end up leaving you, you don't know if you'll be able to live through it."

Her eyes welled.

"I thought that about my sister. That I couldn't live through her dying. But then I met you, and Ashley and your mom, and somehow, instead of dwelling on how much I missed my sister, I starting thinking about how much I loved her. How much I love all of you."

"You don't love us. Especially not me. You hate me, and I hate y-you. Nobody loves me. Not even Mom. Because I'm mean all the time. And I'm sorry, but I can't help it. I feel mean."

"That's okay. Everyone has days they don't feel so nice."

"Wh-why did my dad have to die? How come Honey had to, too? And what if Mom dies, or Ashley? Gramma and Grandpa? And Taffy?"

By the light of the rising moon, Gage helplessly watched on while Lexie's tears began to fall. He knew there was nothing to do to stop her pain, but cradling her against him, he tried his damnedest to ease it.

"I know it hurts," he crooned against the crown of her baby-soft hair. "Let it out. Let all of it out."

He'd never heard anyone cry harder—hadn't known it was possible to cry so hard. Through it all, he held her, rocked her, told her everything would be better. Would it? Who knew. But he had to say something, and that was the only thing that felt right.

"M-Mister Gage?" she finally asked once the worst of her tears subsided. Her voice was unbearably small and quiet. As if pain had reduced her to a shadow of her former self.

"Uh-huh?"

"Please," she whispered, "don't leave."

"I won't, Tater Tot."

"Promise?"

Chest tight, he couldn't fathom what to next say, so he nodded.

What was it with his girls wanting him to make promises he couldn't keep? Or, on this one, could he? It would be so easy to stay. To ask Jess to marry him, and become a true dad to the girls. But would that be fair to them? He hadn't even been able to properly care for his sister. How was he supposed to now take care of a passel of women and horses and even a mangy old, half-blind dog?

Chapter Fourteen

"Everything okay?" Jess asked, stunned to find Lexie cradled on Gage's lap, him stroking her hair.

"Yeah," he said, voice gruff. Had he been crying? His red-rimmed eyes suggested he had. "I'm thinking everything's going to be fine."

"All right...." She glanced over her shoulder to find Doc exiting the clinic, Ashley's slight form in his arms. "Ready to go? Doc said he'd, um, take care of everything from here."

"Lex," he asked, "you ready to head back to the house?"

She nodded against him. "When we get home, will you play Barbies with me? For a long time, they've been wanting to ride in their covered wagon."

"Ah, sure...." He made eye contact with Jess. Eyebrows raised, he appeared as stunned by the girl's behavior as Jess felt. Lexie hadn't even corrected him when he'd shortened her name.

As Gage had ridden with Doc to the clinic, they all squeezed into Jess's pickup. Gage drove with the girls sharing a seat belt in the middle, and Lexie—still sniffling—alongside him. Ashley leaned against Jess, sucking her thumb.

When they reached the dump, Gage parked behind his truck. "Anyone want to ride with me?"

"I will," Lexie said.

Jess and Gage shared another look.

"Thanks, Tater Tot," he said, killing the engine and handing the keys to Jess. "We'll meet back up with you in a few…."

She nodded.

Once they'd exited the truck, Jess stayed long enough to ensure Gage's truck started, then turned the ignition on her own vehicle.

"Mommy?" Ashley asked, resting her cheek on her shoulder.

"Yes, ma'am?" She flashed her daughter a half smile.

"What's wrong with Lexie? She's acting weird."

"I don't know, sweetie, but I kind of like it."

"Yeah." Ashley poked her thumb back into her mouth.

At the house, Jess realized she'd forgotten to turn off the oven. The pork chops were blackened. Great. Just what the night needed was more wonderful news.

"What's that smell?" Ashley asked.

"Dinner." Jess pulled out a chair at the table, and practically fell into it. Exhaustion didn't begin to describe the defeat snaking through her.

"What stinks?" Lexie, followed by Gage, wrinkled her nose.

Jess crossed her arms, resting her head against the back of the chair.

Gage opened the oven door only to blanch. "Whoa."

"What are we going to eat now?" Ashley whined. "I'm starving. Can we have ice cream? Honey loved ice cream."

"True," Jess said with a faint smile, recalling a late

fall day when Ash had been in the barn, licking an ice cream cone, and Honey had gobbled it out of her hand. At the time, Ashley had shrieked, but seeing the strawberry ice cream coating Honey's nose soon enough had her laughing.

"Tell you what," Gage said, "how about we all pile in my truck and go out to eat? Ice cream? Pizza? Steak? You name it. Whatever sounds good."

"I can't afford that," Jess said.

"Who said anything about you paying?" Kissing the top of her head, he said, "Come on, girls, help me get your mom out of this chair and into some fancier duds."

AN HOUR LATER, they were seated in a black leather booth at the nicest place in town, and had just been served their drinks. There should have been smiles all around, but considering what they'd been through, it was a wonder they were even upright.

"What's everyone want?" Gage asked, trying to lighten the mood. "Steak, shrimp—anything on the menu."

"I'm not hungry," Ashley said.

"Can I just have ice cream?" Lexie asked.

"Sure," Gage said. "How about you?" he asked Jess.

"You know, I would think I wouldn't be hungry, either, but I'm starving. The steak and shrimp sounds delicious, but it's too pricey."

He waved off her concern, signaling a tall, skinny waiter. "When you get a chance, we'll take two steak-and-shrimp platters, and three or four bowls of ice cream."

"Any particular flavors?" the waiter asked.

"Lexie?" Gage deferred to her.

"Do you have chocolate?" she asked. "And strawberry?"

"Coming right up."

"Mommy?" Ashley sat so close to Jess she was practically on her lap. "Do you think Honey's with Daddy?"

"I'd like to think so."

"Gage?" the little girl asked. "Do you think so, too?"

"I do," Lexie said. "And Mister Gage's sister's there, too."

"Thanks, for that." The look Gage and her daughter shared was on a level Jess didn't understand. Whatever they'd talked about must have been deep.

"You know what might be nice?" Jess suggested.

"What's that?" Gage, bless his heart, had at least responded. The girls looked ready to start in again with their tears.

"How about we take turns sharing our favorite times with Honey?"

"I'll start," Ashley said. "Remember the time Honey stuck his nose in the water bucket, and he sloshed it all around?"

"That *was* awfully cute," Lexie said as she sipped from her cola. "I liked it when he used to roll in the grass, rubbing his back, and his little legs would stick up…."

Jess sighed. "I've had a lot of horses, but he was by far the one with the most personality."

Toying with his straw wrapper, Gage said, "I was out checking fences one day while you gals were at school, and I'd packed a sandwich, and that rascal snatched it right out of my saddlebag. Ate my chips, too."

"He loved to eat…." Crying again, Ashley hid under her mother's arm. "How come he loved to eat, 'cause if he didn't, he wouldn't have…"

Holding her girl close, Jess patted her back, trying to calm her down.

"Here you go," the waiter said, his give-me-a-big-tip smile not really meshing with the mood. "Um, is everything all right?"

"Yeah," Gage said, handing the girls their ice creams.

"Holler if you need anything."

Ha. What Jess needed was a new life. One where people and pets she loved didn't die. Too bad for her, such a thing didn't exist.

THAT NIGHT, JESS HAD already tucked in Ashley, and was now perched on the edge of Lexie's bed. The only light spilled from the hall, and all was quiet save for the faint sounds of music coming from the movie playing downstairs. "It's been quite a day, huh?"

The girl nodded, then yawned. "I'm really tired."

"I don't blame you."

"Mom?"

"Yep?" Jess pulled up Lexie's covers, snugly fitting them around her. Her cast was gone, her arm fully healed, making the nightly ritual easy again, now that Jess didn't have to be so careful.

"I'm sorry."

"For what?" Jess sat back, skimming hair from the girl's eyes.

"Treating you and Ashley so bad. Mister Gage helped figure out what's been wrong with me."

"He did?"

"Yeah." She twirled a few curls. "We talked about Daddy. And Mister Gage's sister who died. He's real sad about it, and I think he gets how I feel about Daddy. I should've been nicer to him."

"He understands why you weren't," Jess said.

"I hope so…." She bowed her head. "Because now

that we're kinda friends, maybe I don't hate him so much."

Winding her way downstairs, it occurred to Jess that maybe Doc had been right about Honey having died for a reason. She couldn't have fathomed that such a tragedy could bring about a full-fledged miracle, but whatever Gage and Lex had shared had apparently meant the world to her little girl. And that, in turn, meant the world to Jess.

"How is she?" Gage asked, glancing up from the movie.

"I'm not sure how, but all in all, pretty amazing. What did you say to her when you were outside the clinic, sitting in the back of my truck?"

He shrugged. "Truthfully, I don't even remember. I was just so damned sad, and so was she, and we pretty much poured our hearts out and did a lot of sloppy crying."

Sitting sideways on the sofa beside him, she asked, "Was it awful, finding Honey like that on your own?"

"The worst. I was so afraid for the girls. Especially Lex. I couldn't imagine how she was going to take it, especially hearing the news from me."

"Apparently, your delivery method is top-notch."

"Ha-ha." Cupping her cheek, he said, "For a while, with Lex, it was touch and go. But then she started crying—bawling, really. From there, bringing her back to the land of the living seemed pretty much out of my hands."

"Wow." Leaning back, shaking her head, she said, "You remember a while back when we were talking about Lex, and how I mentioned how long it'd been since she'd cried?"

"Sure."

"Well, could it be that simple? That she had so much grief and fear balled up inside her that she could barely cope?"

He shrugged. "I suppose that makes as much sense as any other theory. Who really knows what goes on inside of a kid's mind." He paused, then asked, "Mind if I ask you a favor?"

"After what you did for Lexie, ask anything."

"If you ever tell this to one of my hard-core rodeo friends, I'll deny it, but—" his slow, sad grin tumbled her stomach "—I could seriously use a hug."

IN THE THREE WEEKS since Honey's death, Jess learned to appreciate all over again why she loved living in a small town. Word had spread about the colt's passing, and her mother and Martha's church had formed a posse of sorts to track down the person responsible for dumping the broken glass.

In asking around, they managed to get word through the grapevine of a couple of prime suspects. Waiting for the culprit to strike again, they took turns either staking out the dump site, or going through trash that'd been left, searching for some form of ID. One day, they'd come up lucky, and the sheriff had made an arrest. Swift judgment had been handed down, and Cody Wilder was charged with illegal dumping. He not only had to serve the maximum penalty of thirty days jail time, but also pay a five-thousand-dollar fine. In addition, he had to make restitution for the colt's market value, and clean up the dump site. Having the life of a dear friend and pet reduced to monetary value was a small comfort, but at least it was something. For if the man had gotten away with his crime, Honey's death would have forever haunted Jess.

"Hey, gorgeous." Jess glanced up from the bills she'd been paying at the desk in the den to see Gage in all of his handsome glory.

"Hey, yourself. What's up?"

"I finished sooner than I'd planned in getting that porch rail fixed, and I thought I might persuade you to play hooky."

"Oh, yeah?" Turning in the ancient leather desk chair, she asked, "What do you have in mind?"

"I heard that new Will Ferrell comedy we've been wanting to see is playing over in Lakewood. I took the liberty of checking times, and if we leave this second, we'll make it home just before the girls get off their bus."

Shutting down the computer, she said, "You don't have to twist my arm. Let's go."

During the thirty-minute ride to the neighboring town, Jess couldn't help but let her mind drift to the fact that Gage had called the ranch *home*.

"What's got you so deep in thought?" he asked midway through the trip.

"You'd think it silly," she said, noting that the Jensons had painted their barn. The traditional bright red with white trim looked idyllic against their pasture's bright green.

"Try me," he suggested with a sideways glance in her direction.

"You called the ranch *home*. As in, a place where you feel safe and welcome."

"And?" His grin was contagious.

"And…I just thought it notable."

He shook his head. "Women. Y'all mull over the damnedest things."

"Excuse me, but I think it's important. I want you to

be comfortable with us." Truthfully, she wanted much more from him, but that would hopefully come in time. As it was, the fact that he'd invited her to a movie constituted their first official date.

"You're quiet again," he said, turning left on the paved county road. "Makes me suspicious."

"Good," she teased. "I've always wanted to be a woman of mystery."

Rolling his eyes, they continued their banter all the way to the theater. After paying for tickets, Gage also sprung for buttered popcorn and Milk Duds and Reese's Pieces and two large Cokes. The bill was enormous.

"Want to go Dutch?" she asked.

"Nah. In Texas, it's customary for a man to pay for his woman."

"Is that what I am?" she couldn't resist asking. "*Your* woman?"

"In a manner of speaking." Holding open the door to the dimly lit theater, he smiled.

Great, Jess thought as he led her to a center row seat. One more thing to ponder in regard to where the two of them stood. Aside from the man she'd married, Jess had only dated two other guys. Meaning, her experience with the opposite sex was sorely lacking. Everything in her screamed that Gage was as attracted to her as she was to him. Shoot, he'd as much as admitted the fact, so why wouldn't he act on it?

All through the movie, she ached for him to hold her hand, put his arm around her, or maybe even steal a kiss. But darn it all, he did none of that. Aside from the occasional brush of their legs, she might as well have been sitting alone. Her awareness for the man had her so distracted, she could hardly pay attention to the movie.

When it was over, Jess and Gage filed out of the theater behind other couples. Some holding hands, some kissing, some leaning in while talking. A pang of longing for that kind of intimacy tore through her.

"How're we doing on time?" Gage asked. "We still on schedule to get home for the girls?"

"Yep." However, as for the amount of time it was taking him to get down to the business of wooing her, he'd fallen way behind!

"WHAT DO YOU THINK?" Jess asked a few days later.

"'Bout what?" Seeing how Gage was currently under Jess's truck, changing the oil, he couldn't say as he was thinking about much of anything other than the fact that he hated working on cars.

"My toes, silly."

He glanced to his right to find her wriggling her cute tootsies in a pair of open-toed leather sandals. Wolf-whistling, he said, "They look like a parade of ladybugs."

"Thanks. I think. Is that a good thing?"

"Sure. They've always been my favorite bug."

"Almost done?" she asked.

"I wish." He grunted while ratcheting a particularly crotchety nut.

"Oh." Even from under the truck, her sullen tone told him he'd given the wrong answer.

"Why? Did you have something more fun in mind?"

"Sort of, but if you're busy, we'll do it another time."

"What was it?"

"Just a picnic, but like I said, it's no biggie to postpone. It's just such a pretty day, I thought it might be fun."

"That it would," he said, "but I'm swamped. Rain check?"

"Um, sure." Once she set off with those pretty toes of hers crunching gravel, Gage felt like an A-1 jerk. Any fool could see Jess had been coming on to him in her own, shy way. Just like when they'd been at the movies, she'd kept leaning toward his seat. Again, just like at the movies, he'd wanted nothing more than to pull her against him for a nice, long, wholly satisfying lip-lock session. But seeing as he'd vowed to steer clear of the woman, he couldn't very well turn around and have his way with her.

What he needed to do from here on out was avoid her. If she so much as batted those long, gorgeous eyelashes at him, he'd turn tail and run.

"Gage?"

Just hearing his name on her lips made him flinch, which in turn, caused him to conk his head on the underbelly of the truck's front fender. "Crap, that hurt."

"Slide out from under there, and let me see," she said, kneeling. Too bad for him, she wore a sundress with those sandals of hers, and seeing how he was currently flat on his back, the view was scandalously fine.

"I'm good," he said, ducking back under the truck, willing down the pressure under his fly.

"Don't be stubborn. What if you're bleeding?"

"I'm not. What're you doing back out here? Forget something?"

"I forgot to give you this…." She handed him a sweating glass of iced tea.

"Um, thanks."

"You're welcome."

"Was there something else?" he asked, praying she'd take her slim ankles and sexy-as-hell calves to some other part of the ranch.

"Aren't you at least going to get out from under there long enough to share your drink with me?"

Think fast...

What he needed was a plausible reason as to why he didn't want to share. Something not rude, but understandable. Noble, even.

"Come on," she urged. "Get out from under there."

He coughed. "I, um, would, but I think I'm coming down with something. I'd hate for you to get it."

Sighing, shifting her weight from one leg to the other, she said, "If I didn't know better, I'd swear you were avoiding me."

"Now, why would I go and do a fool thing like that?" he asked, then went back to his task.

"I don't know," she said, "you tell me."

"Tell you what... Soon as I have an answer, you'll be the first to know."

"THIS IS GAGE." A sexual-tension-filled week later, he was outside on a ladder, avoiding Jess while screwing sections of fallen gutter back onto the house. Though no one had said anything, ever since coming across Honey, and not having had his cell, he'd been fanatical about keeping it with him ever since. Doc had assured him that even if he'd called right away, that wouldn't have stopped the colt from being in trouble. But maybe then, at least, there wouldn't be heaviness in his chest, and questions in his heart.

"Long time no hear, buddy." It was his manager, King Lovetz. "I was beginning to think you'd fallen off the planet."

"No such luck." Gage rested his cordless screwdriver on the metal roof, wishing the sky didn't look quite so ominous. "What can I do for you?"

"For starters, get your ass back to Dallas. Everyone's wondering where you've been."

"Right here in Okalahoma, where I told you." Tilting his neck and holding the phone between his ear and shoulder, he took another screw from his tool belt.

"You also told me you'd be back in mid-March, and here it is, pushing April."

"What's it matter?"

"What it matters is that if you have any intention of joining up with the tour, organizers want you back on board…like, yesterday. We all know you had a tough time losing Marnie, Gage, but you can't hide forever. Sooner, or later, you're going to have to get back out there, and do what you were born to do."

Closing his eyes, Gage wished he were in the position to grace his manager with a nice, slow, sarcastic round of applause. The guy was a jerk. He'd always cared more about his bottom line than the emotional well-being of his clients. He was a shark, which at first, had been what had attracted Gage to the guy. But now? Oh, hell, who was he fooling? The thought of getting back on a bull turned his stomach. He had responsibilities. What if he got hurt, and Jess and the girls were left out here to fend for themselves?

Since when did they become your responsibility? his conscience asked.

It was a good question.

One he had no intention of answering.

"Hey, man?" King prompted. "You there?"

"Yeah, but in about thirty seconds, I won't be. I've got stuff to do."

"Don't we all. I want you back in training, Gage. *Now.*"

"Sorry, boss, but no can do." Pressing the off button on his phone, Gage shoved it in his rear pocket.

Thunder rolled, and he stuck the screw in the gutter's slot, twisting it firmly into place. He wanted to finish before the storm. More importantly, he wanted hard work to erase the memory of King's call.

Which is why when it rang again, he ignored it.

"Lemonade?"

Cringing, Gage peered down to find Jess standing alongside the ladder, a tall drink in her hand. She wore another sundress, this one cut low in the front. Instantly aroused, he averted his gaze from her all-too-visible assets. Her red curls hung all loose and wavy, making his fingertips itch from wanting to skim them back to bare a kissable spot on her neck.

"Climb down from there and tell me if this is any good." Wagging the glass, the ice tinkled. "There was a sale on lemons at the grocery store, so I picked some up, thinking I'd make lemonade for the girls."

"For the girls, huh?" On the ground beside her, he accepted the glass, taking a good, long swig.

"Well?" She grinned up at him expectantly. "Is it any good? I haven't made it in years."

With his free hand, he clutched his throat while making a choking sound.

"Stop," she said, giving him a swat.

"Relax. It's delicious." He took another drink. "Thanks for letting me be your guinea pig."

Thunder rolled again, this time, sounding closer.

"I just checked radar," Jess said, "and it looks like we're in for a gullywasher."

"Think the girls will beat it home?"

"No. But with any luck, it'll pass before they're even on the bus."

"Do me a favor," he asked, "and take this for me while I put up my tools."

"Sure, I'll do you a favor," she quipped, taking the glass. "But when am I going to get one?"

Crouching to set his few tools in a wooden-handled open box, he asked, "What do you want?"

Lightning struck, and the resulting thunder shook the ground.

"For one—" she gazed toward the grayish-green sky "—I'd like to get inside before we get struck by lightning."

"That's easy enough. Go on in. Just as soon as I put up the tools and ladder, I'm right behind you."

"Hurry," she called over her shoulder.

"Will do."

Ladder in one hand, toolbox in the other, Gage hustled to the barn. He'd just hung the ladder on its hook when the rain started. At first, just a few fat drops hit the tin roof, but that soon enough changed to hail.

Earlier Jess had put the horses in their stalls. Judging by the snorts and neighs, the weather was making them antsy.

The barn's rolling side doors were open, and gazing out across the yard brought Gage back to the snowstorm. Already, a good inch of nickel-size hail had fallen, transforming red dirt to white.

Jess stood on the house's front porch, shouting something, but he couldn't make out her words above the racket of hail pounding the roof.

"What?" he cried, cupping his hands to his ears.

She laughed, and even through the hail, the sight of her was so pretty, he couldn't stay away.

Ducking his head, he charged into the storm, ignoring the hailstones pounding his back.

"Gage," Jess cried, "go back!"

Laughing and wincing, Gage kept right on running and slipping until reaching his end goal. Jess. Pretty and dry and laughing along with him.

"You're crazy," she said, hands in his dripping hair. "What's wrong with you? Going out in the hail like that?"

"I missed you," he said, meaning every word. Something about talking with King had reminded him how temporary this job was. Only somewhere along the line, his time at the ranch had stopped being a job, and started being his life.

"I—I missed you, too," she said, her voice barely audible above the hail's rattle and roar.

"Hi…" He eased his hands around her waist, holding her as if they were in a slow dance.

"Hello…"

"You smell good. Like lemons and sugar and the barest hint of sweat."

"Sweat?" She tried tugging free, but he held firm. "That's awful. I put deodorant on this morning. Promise."

"It's not that kind of sweat…." Nuzzling her neck, ignoring his conscience screaming at him to run, he sampled her salty goodness.

"Mmm…" she said with a giggle. "That tickles."

If that was her only problem, compared to him, she was getting off easy. What she unwittingly did to him was excruciating—in a good way. But torture all the same. He kissed a ring around to the adorable indentation at the base of her neck. *Stop,* his inner voice railed. Again, Gage ignored it, blazing a trail up the smooth column of her throat, her chin, and finally, deliciously, to her lips. "We shouldn't be doing this," he said.

"I know," she whispered.

Losing himself in every stroke of her tongue, he closed his eyes, drinking her in.

All around them, the storm raged on.

Inside, the battle within him grew equally strong. He'd promised himself he wouldn't do this again. How many times did he have to remind himself that Jess was too good for him?

So what was he doing still kissing her like there was no tomorrow? Chest tight, it was then he finally got it. For them, anyway, there wasn't a tomorrow. Yes, despite King's wishes, Gage might still be on the ranch in the morning, but one day—soon—he'd have to go. Regardless of the fact that the mere thought of leaving was killing him.

Chapter Fifteen

"I asked you once to make love to me," Jess said, pushing away so that even with the rain, he clearly heard her every word. She wanted there to be no misunderstanding. "I appreciate the fact that you're a gentleman more than you know, Gage, but I'm not some love-struck teen. I know what I'm doing."

"Do you?" When she slid her damp, clinging dress over her head, only to toss it onto the wood-planked porch floor, he swallowed hard.

"Who's the boss?" she asked, a smile tugging the corners of her mouth. Her lacy white bra and panties were criminally hot.

"Don't."

"What? Don't fight for what I want?" Hands at her back, she unhooked her bra. "I've been alone for so long, I'd begun to think loneliness was normal. Natural, even. But it's not. With you, I feel happy and sad and tingly and alive and I want to cry and laugh and throttle you and kiss you, and—"

"You're so beautiful," he said, pulling her to him, skimming his fingertips along her spine. "Being with you makes me feel good. Complete."

"Then stay. Forever."

For a few unbearably long seconds, he just stared at her, then asked, "Did you just propose to me?"

Laughing, crying, she nodded. "I—I think I did. Is that all right?" When he'd first come to the ranch, all she'd wanted was for him to be gone, but now, she only wanted him to stay. "What do you think? Because right about now, an answer would be great." Hands to her forehead, uncaring of her near-naked state, she rambled on, "I mean, I just took off my dress in broad daylight, and popped the question, and—"

"I'd like nothing more than to marry you, Jess Cummings."

"You would?" Jess asked. Then how come there'd been that slight rise at the end of his sentence? Like there might've been a *but* coming, but he was too polite to leave her hanging? What if there had been? Did she really want to know? So what if he had doubts? She'd make it her number-one priority to make them all go away. Just in case, she upped the passion in their latest kiss. When she got through with him, he wouldn't know what hit him. He'd be so in love with her, he wouldn't even be able to comprehend letting her go.

LIFTING JESS into his arms, Gage kissed her before carrying her inside, up the stairs, and settling her on her bed. The whole while, he kept asking himself *why?* Why break his every gentlemanly vow to steer clear of Jess for one afternoon of pleasure?

Why? Simple. Because he had no choice. He wanted her—all of her—so damned bad that he ached. Physically, emotionally and every other way in between.

"I love you," he said on a ragged whisper, peeling his wet T-shirt up his chest and over his head only to toss it to the floor.

"I love you, too," she said, a hint of a smile lighting her eyes. In the dim light, she was an angel. *His* angel.

"How much time do we have before the girls get home from school?"

"Enough…" Holding out her arms to him, she said, "Come here. Kiss me. And get that scowl off your face. This is supposed to be fun."

"Sorry," he said with a grimace, covering the truth behind his mixed-up mood. "It's been a while."

"You think it hasn't for me?" Her laugh shot through him.

"I don't even have a condom."

"Seeing how I'd love nothing more than to have your child growing inside me, I fail to see how that's a problem."

A child? Good Lord, what was he doing? This had to stop—now. Kissing her as sweetly and urgently as he knew how, he pushed off the bed, then covered her with the pale yellow sheet.

With his back to her, staring out the window at the rain, he scrubbed his hands over his face.

"Gage? Sweetie, what's wrong?"

Turning to face her, he said, "You know I love you, right?"

"I—I think I do. I mean, you've told me, but…" She, too, left the bed, but paid no heed to the sheet he'd draped over her beautiful curves. Crossing the short distance to him, she was all woman, wearing nothing but her panties and a concerned smile. "Look at you," she said, tracing the outline of one of his many, angry rodeo scars. "Is this why you're having a hard time being with me? Because you're embarrassed about these?"

No. Hell, no, he wasn't embarrassed about what in

another life he'd labeled his badges of honor. The scars that consumed him with shame were the ones on the inside. The ones that apparently no amount of love and care would ever fade.

When she pressed her small, soft hands against his chest, then proceeded to kiss the raised line over his ribs where he'd last been gored, it was his undoing.

Groaning, he hefted her up, urging her legs around his waist. After kissing her, he set her atop an antique dresser, fumbling with her panties. "We need these off," he murmured, hating himself, loving her. Quickly processing what needed to be done, he lifted her again, this time setting her feet to the ground. Kneeling before her, he slid the lacy scrap down, kissing every inch of the skin he'd bared.

A glance upward showed her neck arched, her eyes closed. Once her panties were off, he pulled down his jeans, taking his boxers along with them.

Skimming his fingertips along her hourglass form, he rose, easing splayed fingers into the hair at the back of her head. The band holding her ponytail in place snapped, cascading her curls into a lush curtain for her breasts. The peekaboo effect nearly destroyed him. "You're perfect," he said, kissing her throat.

"So are you…."

No. Nowhere close, but for the moment, anyway, guiding her back to the bed, he unwisely chose to ignore that fact. He chose instead to pretend that they were married, and that pleasures like this were the norm instead of a once-in-a-lifetime treat.

Lying beside her, rain pounding the tin roof, sealing them in their own world, he traced her jaw, her nose, the lush swell of her breasts. He committed every inch of her to memory, as all too soon, that's all he'd have of her.

"Stop teasing me," she said, sadly having no clue as to the gravity of the situation. Plunging her fingers into his hair, she coaxed him into a kiss. The bold sweep of her tongue and gyrating of her hips left no doubt as to what she had on her mind. "I need you inside me—now."

"Slow down," he urged, needing this to last. Needing the memory of her to stay with him a lifetime.

"We'll have plenty of time to go slow later." Straddling him, Jess winked. "All the time in the world. Right now, cowboy, I just want to ride."

Sensation shot through her. Hot and shining. Vibrant in its intensity.

Gripping the iron bedstead, it was all Jess could do to keep from crying out. She'd thought she'd never be gifted with physical pleasure again, but Gage had given her that, plus so much more.

"I love you," she said a while later, snuggling against him, resting her cheek against his chest. "For the first time, since…you know, I feel safe and secure and adored."

He said nothing, just kissed her forehead, gently tucking stray curls behind her ears.

"The girls feel the same. We all love you, Gage, and just as soon as possible, I think we should have our wedding. Nothing fancy. A small church ceremony with our closest family and friends."

When he said nothing, just silently stroked her spine, she'd have given anything to fall into a deep, dark hole. She hadn't just voiced that fantasy aloud, had she?

Heat—no longer the good kind—crept up her neck and cheeks.

"Gage?"

"Mmm-hmm?"

"Y-you know I was joking, right? I mean, we love you, but that other stuff... That would be rushing things." She blasted him with a smile. "Funny, huh?"

He kissed her cheek, then said, "If I'm going to beat the school bus, I need to get out of here."

TO SAY THAT MAKING love with Gage had been amazing would be the understatement of the century. More than anything, as Jess stood under the shower's spray, she wished the girls weren't due home any minute. That way, she and Gage could be showering together and talking about that awkward silence instead of him having had to rush off to the bunkhouse to protect her *honor.* More to the point, neither of them had thought it appropriate for the girls to find them in a delicate situation.

Toweling dry, Jess frowned, but then grinned.

What was wrong with her?

She and Gage had just made love. *Made love!*

As for Gage's silence, there were times when he was a deep guy. She tended to overanalyze and needed to stop. He was a good man. Her singing heart told her that was all she needed to know.

Outside, the storm had passed.

Off to the east, thunder still rolled, but over the ranch, the sun now shone. A good omen? Tugging on clean panties, a bra, jeans and a T-shirt, she'd like to think so.

Was Gage whistling in the shower, as happy about what had just transpired as her? Had he been put off by her take-charge bedroom manner? She hoped not. While she'd appreciated his painful politeness, enough was enough. In him, she'd seen something she very much wanted and had decided to, quite literally, take matters into her own hands.

Grinning, she padded barefoot downstairs, aiming for the kitchen. A quick glance at the clock over the stove showed she still had about five minutes before the girls got home. Damn. She could have showered with Gage after all.

Oh, well… Better safe than sorry.

In the freezer, she searched for just the right thing for dinner. She wanted something hearty, but a little fancy to let him know she cared. Beef tips seemed right, so she grabbed a pound of chopped beef, then popped it in the microwave to thaw.

"Mooo-ooom!" Ashley came bounding into the room.

"Hey, cutie," Jess said, pulling her into a hug. "Have a happy day?"

"Uh-huh, and look what I made." She took a picture from her backpack. With elbow macaroni, she'd made a ship, sailing on a split-pea sea.

"Whoa," Jess said, "that's seriously nice."

"Thanks. Can I put it on the fridge?"

"Sure." While Ashley took her time picking a magnet, Jess fished egg noodles from the cabinet and peas from the freezer. "Where's Lexie?"

"She's comin'. First, she had to give Mister Gage the art project she made for him."

"What is it?"

"A supercool flower shirt. She made it out of paper plates, and painted it yellow."

"Wow…" Grinning, Jess couldn't wait to see Gage flouncing around in that. And because of the great father he was going to make, he'd not only put it on, but would also be proud wearing it.

The back door slammed. "Mo-om!" Lexie hollered.

"I'm right here, sweetie. What's up?"

"Do you know where Gage is? I made this for him, but I can't find him anywhere." She held out a shirt that resembled sunshine-yellow armor with sections of paper plate sewn together with yellow yarn.

"It's, um, gorgeous," Jess said, more excited than ever to see Gage all dolled up. "Did you try the barn?"

"Uh-huh." Lex grabbed an apple from the fridge.

"The bunkhouse?"

"Kinda. But it was dark, so I didn't go in."

Frowning, Jess took the meat from the microwave, turning it before nuking it again. "Wonder where he could be…."

"I dunno. But his truck's gone. Maybe he went to the feed store?"

"Hmm." The meat had another six minutes until it was ready, so Jess offered to round him up herself. No doubt he'd probably seen one of their new colts straying too far, and had gone after him in the truck instead of taking the time to saddle Henrietta. "Be right back," she said. "While I'm gone, Lex, could you please chop an onion?"

"'Kay."

The difference in Lexie was nothing short of miraculous. No matter what he said, Jess credited Gage with her daughter's amazing changes.

Outside, the air smelled fresh-washed after the rain. The passing front had left in its wake cooler air, with much less humidity.

"Gage?" Jess hollered, hands framing her mouth.

Sure enough, his truck was gone, but considering the intimacies they'd just shared, there had to be a plausible explanation.

Head tipped back, eyes closed while drinking in the sun, Jess touched her hands to flushed cheeks.

Opening her eyes, Jess set off for the bunkhouse. He had three distinct sets of boots—work boots, riding boots and dress boots. Judging by which pair was gone, she'd be able to pinpoint his exact location.

With the shades drawn, the bunkhouse was darker than usual. "Gage?"

When he didn't answer, she flipped on the lights, only to fight a rush of nausea.

The bed had been stripped. The quilt neatly folded, Gage's two pillows on top. Tossing open the bathroom door, she found dirty towels and the sheets in the tub, as if the bunkhouse—the ranch—had been nothing more than one of the hotels he'd stayed at while on the road.

Back in the main room, she found a slip of paper on the dresser.

Pulse racing, her mouth like cotton, she read:

Jess—words can't say how sorry I am for doing this to you and the girls, but here goes. First, please don't ever think I don't love you, Ashley and Lex, because I do. Trouble is, I've got a past I haven't shared with you, and it's ugly. This afternoon, when you told me I make you feel safe, my past came rushing back to remind me that in being happy with you, I've been living a lie. For what I've done, I don't deserve happiness. I had no right to make promises to Lexie, and I never meant to make love to you, and I should be sorry for our act, but truthfully, I'm not. For the rest of my life, I'll close my eyes at night and wake in the morning to my memories of all of you. Love always—Gage

Releasing a frustrated groan, Jess crumpled the note into a wad. BS—that's what Gage's words had been.

He loved her? Ha!

How could he make such a claim, have made such unbearably sweet love to her, then leave her with nothing more than a stupid note? Such an act wasn't one of love, but of selfishness, and she'd be damned if she'd let him get away with it.

Whatever this deep, dark secret he'd often alluded to was, it was high time he let her in on it.

And if he didn't?

Forcing a deep breath, Jess reasoned she'd cross that bridge when—if—she got to it. In the meantime, her primary goal was to find him, then give him a major piece of her mind.

Chapter Sixteen

"Did you find him?" Lexie stood at the kitchen counter, chopping away on the onion Jess had assigned her to dice for dinner. "I hope so, because I worked *really* hard on his shirt."

"You know," Jess said, swallowing the knot in her throat, "I did find him, only he had to leave right away."

"Why?" Ashley asked, munching an oatmeal cream pie. Cream lined her upper lip, giving her a white mustache. She looked adorable. Best of all, oblivious to the turmoil churning her mother's stomach.

"Family emergency," Jess said, reaching for the phone.

Ashley looked up. "Who're you calling?"

"Grandma. I forgot an ingredient in my dinner recipe."

"When's Gage coming back?" Lexie asked.

"Soon, sweetie." *If I have anything to say about it, very, very soon.*

Punching in her parents' number, not wanting the girls to hear her call, Jess hid out in the living room. After quickly relaying the situation—leaving out the portion of the afternoon where she and Gage had made love—Georgia promised to be right over.

After checking to make sure the girls weren't listening, Jess next dialed Doc. Only from him, after explaining the basics, she demanded answers. "So, tell me, Doc, if you wanted to find that miserable scum, where would you first look?"

GAGE SWATTED AN empty beer can from his sofa, then fell onto the leather cushions. From a trash-cluttered side table, he took the remote, turning on his flat-screen television. After flipping through two hundred-plus channels and finding nothing to watch, he turned off the TV in favor of another nap.

He'd been home barely twelve hours, but was already bored and lonely.

The room's only light was a side table lamp. The place was trashed with all of his gear having been dumped by the door, and fast food and junk food remains strewn over the tables. What could he say? In times of crisis, a man had to eat.

Leaving Jess and the girls had been impossibly hard, but what other option did he have?

Still, no matter how many times he told himself he'd done the right thing, the ache in his gut told another story.

When a knock sounded on his condo door, he ignored it. No one even knew he was here. That said, when the knocking grew more persistent, he mumbled a string of curses, then undid his locks before jerking open the door. "What? Oh…"

"That all you have to say?" Casting him a look of squinty-eyed fury, Jess brushed past him, inviting herself inside.

"Jess…" Groaning, he covered his face with his hands.

"Don't you dare, *Jess,* me." Jerking his hands from

his face, she snapped, "Don't hide your eyes, either. For what I have to stay, I want every ounce of your attention." Her gaze darted around the room. "Good grief, Gage, your home is a palace. Messy, but… Whoa. What are you? Rich?"

"I do all right." Turning from her, he reclaimed his former spot on the sofa. "Now, if you don't mind, please say what you have to, then kindly leave. I'm busy."

She snorted. "Oh—I can see."

Standing in front of him, hands on her hips, she said, "I'm waiting."

"For what?"

"No." She released a sharp laugh. "You *did not* just say that to me."

"Baby, there's more going on here than you can possibly comprehend, and—"

"First, unless you're prepared to do some awfully fast talking, don't ever call me *baby* again. Second, did some bull gore out your heart, because what you just did in agreeing to marry me, making love to me, telling me you love me, then vanishing, was pretty damned low."

"I already told you… It's complicated."

"Complicated? Gee, would that be the understatement of the decade. So, tell me, Gage, what part of your actions confuses you most? The way you ran out on me? Or the girls? Or the way you lied to me, telling me you love me, when—"

"Let's get one thing right," he said, pushing up from the sofa, positioning himself uncomfortably close. "I do love you. Very much. Which is why I left. To save you from me."

"That's such BS! Liar!"

Turning his back on her, he crossed to a mahogany

storage cabinet, and threw open the door. Inside, he withdrew a scrapbook, only it didn't hold memories of happy times. Tossing it to the coffee table where it slammed into empty bags and cans, he said, "You wanna know the real me? The guy you're damned lucky to be rid of? Take a gander at that...."

"Where are you going?" she asked when he grabbed his ragged cowboy hat from the floor.

"Out."

"Don't even think about it," she said, dragging him to the sofa and pushing him down. "You left me once, Gage, and you're not doing it again."

"What is wrong with you?" he asked. "Why won't you get it through that thick head of yours that I'm no good for you...or your girls?"

"Hush," Jess said, tired of Gage's excuses. Sitting beside him, she reached for the scrapbook he'd dumped on the coffee table. "I'm seriously sick of you telling me what to think about you. I'm a big girl, Gage, and I'll make my own decisions."

Flipping through page after page, picture after picture, introduced her to a fun-loving, smiling female version of Gage. Slowly it dawned on her that the woman must be his sister. Upon reaching her obituary, Jess's suspicions were confirmed.

While Gage sat cross-armed and stone-faced alongside her, the ache in Jess's chest deepened. Finally, she closed the book, turning to Gage to end the heartrending story.

"You haven't finished," he said. "Keep reading, and you'll understand."

"I don't want to *read* what happened to your sister, Gage. I want to hear about it from you."

"I—I can't..." With a violent shake of his head, he

was once again on his feet, this time pacing like a caged animal around the perimeter of the room.

Going to him, hands on his shoulders, she whispered, "Relax. It's just me. You know everything there is to know about my life. I'd appreciate the same courtesy from you." When he said nothing, and his muscles tensed beneath her fingers, she added, "Please, Gage... No matter what happened, it's not my place to judge you. I just want—need—to know."

Refusing to meet her stare, he said in a halting voice, "O-okay." Taking her by the hand, he returned her to the sofa. "M-Marnie was my baby sister. Seven years younger than me, when Mom had her, I thought she was the neatest thing since G.I. Joe—only she had real working limbs and stuff, you know?" He laughed, and in the dim light, his eyes glistened with tears. "Anyway, I loved that girl like crazy. Dad and I always kept a close eye out for her, and in general, approved of the guys she dated. Last time I was on the road, Marnie was a year out of college, in between jobs and boyfriends, and I invited her to tag along. She was good company—even better when she admitted to having a crush on my best bud, Deke." Shaking his head, Gage said, "I loved him like a brother. Nothing made me happier than the two of them as a couple."

When Gage again fell silent, Jess prompted, "That sounds wonderful. Did they marry?"

"No." Jaw hardened, he stared straight ahead, clenching and unclenching his fists. "Once the season ended, she moved in with him. Though I hated the thought of her *shacking up,* I'd had a man-to-man with Deke, and he promised his intentions were to make an honest woman of her. Sounds old-fashioned, I know, but that's just the way I was raised."

"Of course," Jess said, her stomach tense over where this story may be leading. "Me, too."

"Oh, everyone from church to our grandparents thought them the sweetest couple ever. Deke was a charmer." A sarcastic snort escaped him. "Can't count how many times I told him I was pleased he was joining the family. Then Marnie started showing up at birthdays and anniversaries with blackened eyes and bruised cheeks from *running into doors*. A broken wrist from *tripping down the stairs*."

"No…" Jess's throat knotted. "How horrible."

"Thing is, until it was too late, I never suspected a thing. Deke was my best friend. My freakin' best friend. How could I not have seen him for what he was? A monster. One night I headed over there to see if Deke wanted to join me for a quick beer, when I heard y-yelling." Hand to his forehead, he coughed as if he might be sick.

"It's okay. Take your time."

He nodded, then continued. "Everyone fights, you know. I wasn't going to interfere in their private business. Then some old neighbor lady sticks her head out the door, and tells me I'd 'better get in there, or this time he just might kill her.'" Laughing, wiping tears from the corners of his eyes, he said, "Hell, even then I didn't believe. It took Marnie screaming for me to kick in the door. I had to find Deke standing over her with a baseball bat—her face so bruised, I hardly recognized her— to finally figure it out. Wh-when I asked him what the hell he was doing, the bastard came after me."

"Oh, Gage…" Jess edged closer to him, resting her hands on his thigh.

"All I could think was that if I was going to get Marnie out of there, I had to swing at him before he swung at me. I hit him so hard, he fell back, hitting a coffee table's sharp corner. Th-the blow to the back of his head killed him. Paramedics showed. They stabilized Marnie. Asked if I wanted to ride along with her to the hospital. I did, but about midway there, it was too late…."

Jess brushed the tears from her cheeks.

"Authorities deemed Deke's death self-defense on my part. Everyone told me to remember the good times with Marnie and get on with my life. I tried," he said with a mirthless laugh, "but it was no good. That's why I showed up at your ranch. I needed something—anything—to dull the pain, and hard work seemed like the best thing. But then you and the girls kind of took over. I became so focused on all of you, that I forgot to worry about me. But, Jess, after we made love, when you told me how I made you feel safe, don't you see why I had to go? That it was for the best? If it hadn't been for me—for me seeing only what I wanted to—Marnie would still be alive."

Lips pressed tight, Jess shook her head. "Don't *ever* say that again. How could you be to blame when you had no idea what was happening? Your sister was old enough to know she was in over her head. She should've asked you—anyone—for help. You had no more control over what happened with her than we had over that ice storm hitting when you first got to the ranch. In even attempting to save Marnie, you were a hero. Yes, sweetheart, what happened was horrible, but you have to let it go. Why run? Why not let me and the girls help you like you've helped us?" Smoothing her hands over his dear, whisker-stubbled cheeks, she added, "I love you. The girls love you. I appreciate the fact that in leaving, you thought you were doing good, but you were wrong."

Turning to her, clinging to her for dear life, Gage broke down. It may not have been manly, but it couldn't be helped. The dammed-up pain had to bust out.

"It's okay," Jess crooned, smoothing his back. "I love you. Everything's going to be okay."

"I-I'm sorry," he said. "You have to know I didn't want to leave you or the girls, but I had to."

"I know," she said, holding him all the tighter, stroking his hair. "It's okay. Everything's going to be okay."

"I love you," he finally said. "Thank you."

"For what?"

"Being here."

"Always," she reassured. "I may have had to take a gamble on you once, but I know a good thing when I see one, and from the start, Gage Moore, my heart told me you were a keeper."

Sitting up, covering his face with his hands, he groaned. "In leaving, what kind of mess have I made with the girls?"

"None. I covered for you. Told them you had a family emergency."

"Thank you," he said, raining kisses on her cheeks and eyelids and chin. "Thank you, thank you, thank you."

Urging his attention to her lips, she returned his gratitude with appreciation all her own.

Epilogue

"Gage, please?" Lexie looked up at him with those big blue eyes of hers, and as usual, he was powerless to say no.

"All right," he said, giving in to her pleas for barrel-racing lessons even though he knew her momma wanted her inside. In the heat of foaling season, things had been a little crazy around the ranch. After chores, he'd promised to help out with the final preparations for Abby's first-birthday party. "But we're keeping this short. If you're not cleaned up in time for your baby sister's party, it's my behind your mom's going to chew."

"She won't be mad," Lexie reassured.

"Right." Giving his eldest girl an affectionate swat, he steered his future rodeo queen toward Romeo—a gorgeous bay he'd surprised her with on her birthday.

"Gage? Lexie?" Jess, baby Abby in her arms, stood on the front porch hollering.

"Oh, no," Lexie said, chin dragging her chest. "Does this mean we have to go inside to scrub toilets and stuff?"

"'Fraid so," he said, "but how about after the party, we sneak out to run a few barrels?"

"Promise?"

"Yes, ma'am." With a tip of his hat, he gave the girl his most solemn vow. After all, he wasn't in the habit of breaking his word, and he sure wasn't about to start now.

"What was that about?" Jess asked once Lexie had dashed past them to run inside.

He kissed his newest daughter's pretty pink forehead. "Lex was after me to start her barrel racing. As a good parent, what else could I do?"

"Uh-huh." Jess grinned. "You'll do anything to get out of scrubbing commodes, won't you?"

"Can you blame me?" Taking the baby, he breathed her in. Even a year after her birth, he never tired of her perfect scent. Pink lotion and powder and a little extra something that made him want to be the world's most doting father.

"Sweetheart," Jess said with a sigh, "I want everything perfect for your parents."

"It's not like they haven't seen the place before."

"I know, but your mom helped so much in planning the addition that I want everything perfect."

He rolled his eyes. "Miss Abby? Have you ever heard a bigger load of bologna?"

The infant cooed.

"She agrees," Gage teased.

Jess flashed her sweetest smile. "Then she can help clean commodes."

"Woman," Gage said, slipping his arm around her waist before helping himself to a kiss, "anyone ever told you you're a mean boss?"

"All the time. Lucky for you, that if you do a good job, I heard there might be a bonus in it."

"Oh, yeah? What kind of bonus?"

She winked. "If you ever want to find out, looks like you'd better get scrubbing."

* * * * *

Here is a sneak preview of
A STONE CREEK CHRISTMAS,
the latest in Linda Lael Miller's acclaimed
McKETTRICK series.

A lonely horse brought vet Olivia O'Ballivan to
Tanner Quinn's farm, but it's the rancher's love
that might cause her to stay.

A STONE CREEK CHRISTMAS
Available December 2008
from Silhouette Special Edition

Tanner heard the rig roll in around sunset. Smiling, he wandered to the window. Watched as Olivia O'Ballivan climbed out of her Suburban, flung one defiant glance toward the house and started for the barn, the golden retriever trotting along behind her.

Taking his coat and hat down from the peg next to the back door, he put them on and went outside. He was used to being alone, even liked it, but keeping company with Doc O'Ballivan, bristly though she sometimes was, would provide a welcome diversion.

He gave her time to reach the horse Butterpie's stall, then walked into the barn.

The golden retriever came to greet him, all wagging tail and melting brown eyes, and he bent to stroke her soft, sturdy back. "Hey, there, dog," he said.

Sure enough, Olivia was in the stall, brushing Butterpie down and talking to her in a soft, soothing voice that touched something private inside Tanner and made him want to turn on one heel and beat it back to the house.

He'd be damned if he'd do it, though.

This was *his* ranch, *his* barn. Well-intentioned as she was, *Olivia* was the trespasser here, not him.

"She's still very upset," Olivia told him, without turning to look at him or slowing down with the brush.

Shiloh, always an easy horse to get along with, stood contentedly in his own stall, munching away on the feed Tanner had given him earlier. Butterpie, he noted, hadn't touched her supper as far as he could tell.

"Do you know anything at all about horses, Mr. Quinn?" Olivia asked.

He leaned against the stall door, the way he had the day before, and grinned. He'd practically been raised on horseback; he and Tessa had grown up on their grandmother's farm in the Texas hill country, after their folks divorced and went their separate ways, both of them too busy to bother with a couple of kids. "A few things," he said. "And I mean to call you Olivia, so you might as well return the favor and address me by my first name."

He watched as she took that in, dealt with it, decided on an approach. He'd have to wait and see what that turned out to be, but he didn't mind. It was a pleasure just watching Olivia O'Ballivan grooming a horse.

"All right, *Tanner*," she said. "This barn is a disgrace. When are you going to have the roof fixed? If it snows again, the hay will get wet and probably mold…"

He chuckled, shifted a little. He'd have a crew out there the following Monday morning to replace the roof and shore up the walls—he'd made the arrangements over a week before—but he felt no particular compunction to explain that. He was enjoying her ire too much; it made her color rise and her hair fly when she turned her head, and the faster breathing made her perfect breasts go up and down in an enticing rhythm. "What makes you so sure I'm a greenhorn?" he asked mildly, still leaning on the gate.

At last she looked straight at him, but she didn't move from Butterpie's side. "Your hat, your boots—that fancy red truck you drive. I'll bet it's customized."

Tanner grinned. Adjusted his hat. "Are you telling me real cowboys don't drive red trucks?"

"There are lots of trucks around here," she said. "Some of them are red, and some of them are new. And *all* of them are splattered with mud or manure or both."

"Maybe I ought to put in a car wash, then," he teased. "Sounds like there's a market for one. Might be a good investment."

She softened, though not significantly, and spared him a cautious half smile, full of questions she probably wouldn't ask. "There's a good car wash in Indian Rock," she informed him. "People go there. It's only forty miles."

"Oh," he said with just a hint of mockery. "*Only* forty miles. Well, then. Guess I'd better dirty up my truck if I want to be taken seriously in these here parts. Scuff up my boots a bit, too, and maybe stomp on my hat a couple of times."

Her cheeks went a fetching shade of pink. "You are twisting what I said," she told him, brushing Butterpie again, her touch gentle but sure. "I meant…"

Tanner envied that little horse. Wished he had a furry hide, so he'd need brushing, too.

"You *meant* that I'm not a real cowboy," he said. "And you could be right. I've spent a lot of time on construction sites over the last few years, or in meetings where a hat and boots wouldn't be appropriate. Instead of digging out my old gear, once I decided to take this job, I just bought new."

"I bet you don't even *have* any old gear," she challenged, but she was smiling, albeit cautiously, as though she might withdraw into a disapproving frown at any second.

He took off his hat, extended it to her. "Here," he teased. "Rub that around in the muck until it suits you."

She laughed, and the sound—well, it caused a powerful and wholly unexpected shift inside him. Scared the hell out of him and, paradoxically, made him yearn to hear it again.

* * * * *

Discover how this rugged rancher's wanderlust is tamed in time for a merry Christmas, in
A STONE CREEK CHRISTMAS.
In stores December 2008.

Silhouette®

SPECIAL EDITION™

FROM *NEW YORK TIMES* BESTSELLING AUTHOR

LINDA LAEL MILLER

A STONE CREEK CHRISTMAS

Veterinarian Olivia O'Ballivan finds the animals in Stone Creek playing Cupid between her and Tanner Quinn. Even Tanner's daughter, Sophie, is eager to play matchmaker. With everyone conspiring against them and the holiday season fast approaching, Tanner and Olivia may just get everything they want for Christmas after all!

*Available December 2008
wherever books are sold.*

SPECIAL EDITION™

MISTLETOE AND MIRACLES

by *USA TODAY* bestselling author
MARIE FERRARELLA

Child psychologist Trent Marlowe couldn't believe his eyes when Laurel Greer, the woman he'd loved and lost, came to him for help. Now a widow, with a troubled boy who wouldn't speak, Laurel needed a miracle from Trent…and a brief detour under the mistletoe wouldn't hurt, either.

Available in December wherever books are sold.

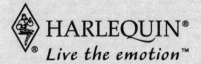

REQUEST YOUR FREE BOOKS!

2 FREE NOVELS PLUS 2
FREE GIFTS!

American ★ Romance®

Love, Home & Happiness!

MERLINE LOVELACE

THE DUKE'S NEW YEAR'S RESOLUTION

Sabrina Russo is touring southern Italy when an accident places her in the arms of sexy Dr. Marco Calvetti. The Italian duke and doctor reluctantly invites her to his villa to heal…and soon after, he is vowing to do whatever he needs to keep her in Italy *and* in his bed….

**Available December
wherever books are sold.**

Always Powerful, Passionate and Provocative.

Harlequin® Historical
Historical Romantic Adventure!

THE MISTLETOE WAGER
Christine Merrill

Harry Pennyngton, Earl of Anneslea, is surprised when his estranged wife, Helena, arrives home for Christmas. Especially when she's intent on divorce! A festive house party is in full swing when the guests are snowed in, and Harry and Helena find they are together under the mistletoe....

Available December 2008 wherever books are sold.

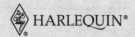

HARLEQUIN®

American ★ *Romance*®

COMING NEXT MONTH

#1237 A BABY IN THE BUNKHOUSE by Cathy Gillen Thacker
Made in Texas
When Rafferty Evans offers the very pregnant Jacey Lambert shelter from a
powerful rainstorm, the Texas rancher doesn't expect to deliver her baby! Now,
with five cowpokes ooh-ing and ahh-ing over the new mom's infant, can Jacey
help the handsome widower open his heart to the love—and instant family—
she's offering?

#1238 ONCE UPON A CHRISTMAS by Holly Jacobs
American Dads
Is Daniel McLean the father of Michelle Hamilton's nephew? As Daniel spends
time with the young Brandon, and helps Michelle organize Erie Elementary's
big Christmas Fair, the three of them come to realize a paternity test won't make
them a family. But the love Michelle and Daniel discover just might…

#1239 A TEXAN RETURNS by Victoria Chancellor
Brody's Crossing
Wyatt McCall just blew back into town, still gorgeous, still pulling outrageous
stunts like the ones he did in high school. And the stunt he's planning this time
around could reunite him with the woman he loves. Mayor Toni Casale, who
still hasn't gotten over Wyatt, has no idea what the Texas bad boy has in store
for Brody's Crossing—and for *her*—this Christmas!

#1240 THE PREGNANCY SURPRISE by Kara Lennox
Second Sons
Sara Kauffman is lively, spontaneous, playful—everything Reece Remington is
not. Although he's only visiting the coastal Texas town where she lives, Reece has
a surprisingly good time helping Sara run a local B&B. Could this buttoned-
down guy be ready for an entirely different kind of surprise?

www.eHarlequin.com

HARCNMBPA1108